"Are you cold, or just nervous?"
Zack asked with a grin.

"Cold," Maddy mumbled, hugging herself and lying with conviction.

"Well, it would help if you came in off my doorstep," Zack said.

Maddy looked around, surprised she was still outside. "Oh." But she stayed where she was until Zack sighed, took her hand, and pulled her inside.

"Come on, Maddy, do I really look like a maniac who drowns blonds in his hot tub? Trust me, you're going to enjoy this."

Zack's mouth had been curved in a smile, but as she gazed at him it seemed to blur and soften. He let go of her hand then and touched her face, drawing his thumb across the film of moisture on her upper lip. Maddy's lips parted in response. He caressed her warm cheek with the backs of his fingers, then delicately lifted a strand of her hair and tucked it behind her ear.

"Maddy . . . close your eyes . . ."

WHAT ARE *LOVESWEPT* ROMANCES?

They are stories of true romance and touching emotion. We
believe those two very important ingredients are constants
in our highly sensual and very believable stories in the
LOVESWEPT line. Our goal is to give you, the reader,
stories of consistently high quality that may sometimes make
you laugh, sometimes make you cry, but are always fresh
and creative and contain many delightful surprises within
their pages.

Most romance fans read an enormous number of books.
Those they truly love, they keep. Others may be traded with
friends and soon forgotten. We hope that each *LOVESWEPT*
romance will be a treasure—a "keeper." We will always try
to publish

*LOVE STORIES YOU'LL NEVER FORGET
BY AUTHORS YOU'LL ALWAYS REMEMBER*

The Editors

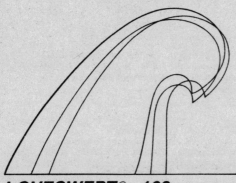

LOVESWEPT® • 163

Kathleen Creighton
Still Waters

BANTAM BOOKS
TORONTO • NEW YORK • LONDON • SYDNEY • AUCKLAND

STILL WATERS

A Bantam Book / November 1986

*LOVESWEPT® and the wave device are registered
trademarks of Bantam Books, Inc. Registered in U.S. Patent
and Trademark Office and elsewhere.*

Cover art by Lino Safiotti.

*If you would be interested in receiving protective vinyl
covers for your Loveswept books, please write to this address
for information:*

Loveswept
Bantam Books
P.O. Box 985
Hicksville, NY 11802

ISBN 0-553-21781-X

Published simultaneously in the United States and Canada

---

*Bantam Books are published by Bantam Books, Inc. Its trade-
mark, consisting of the words "Bantam Books" and the por-
trayal of a rooster, is Registered in U.S. Patent and Trademark
Office and in other countries. Marca Registrada. Bantam
Books, Inc., 666 Fifth Avenue, New York, New York 10103.*

PRINTED IN THE UNITED STATES OF AMERICA

O   0 9 8 7 6 5 4 3 2 1

*This one's for you, Barb,
for all the times you've restored my soul.*

One

Maddy Gordon knew she must be having a nightmare. She'd gone to sleep unawares in San Ramon, California, and awakened in Munchkinland. It was the only explanation. All around her were little heads, ranging in color from palest flaxen to glossy black, and not one of them came more than two inches above her kneecaps. She felt as conspicuous as a giraffe in a pygmy village.

It wasn't too late. She could still change her mind. Furtively, she looked around the huge, murky room, breathing the pungent smell of chlorine while she considered the possibility of escape. She'd managed to put off fulfilling her New Year's resolution until June—no reason why she couldn't put it off a little longer. Like . . . until the *next* New Year.

But no. Maddy took a deep breath and squared her shoulders, resolutely avoiding looking at the glittering expanse of water. She'd made up her mind. No matter what, come hell or high water, this was going to be the year she learned to swim.

She'd been meaning to do it for years, but somehow

she always managed to find a very good reason why it wasn't the right time. But now she was twenty-five, beginning her second quarter-century. It was the kind of milestone that couldn't be ignored. This, she was determined, would be the year she finally faced her unreasoning terror of water and conquered it.

Way back in early spring, when the resolve had been fresh and the reality remote, she had gone down to the San Ramon Parks and Recreation Department to inquire about swimming lessons. The girl at the desk had been accommodating. There were, the girl told her, classes for beginners, advanced beginners, and intermediates; classes in advanced life-saving, synchronized swimming, and scuba diving; classes for moms and babies; and classes for the physically handicapped. Maddy had thanked her and signed up for the beginners' class, at twelve-thirty. The girl hadn't asked about age or thought to tell her that, except for Maddy, the class would consist almost entirely of five-year-olds.

Now Maddy made the mistake of looking out over the gently undulating, iridescent expanse of water. She felt an instantaneous wave of giddiness. She thought that if she could only sit down, she wouldn't feel so huge and ungainly.

Feeling large and awkward wasn't new to her. She was five ten and had achieved most of that height very early. And to make matters worse, height wasn't the only thing she'd acquired early. Some of her most painful memories had to do with her sixth-grade dance class, when most of her partners had been precisely at eye level with her newly emerging bosom. Now, of course, neither her height, proportions, nor Nordic coloring could be considered very remarkable. In this Southern California town she was just another California "golden girl." But only on the outside. On the inside she was still that gawky little girl, embarrassed and dismayed by her own body.

There seemed to be no place to sit except on the

edge of the pool. As much as she yearned to sit down, she wasn't ready for that yet. The thought of it made her shiver and break out in goose bumps, a condition that only intensified her self-consciousness by making her nipples harden and stand out like buttons under the form-fitting racing-style bathing suit she'd bought especially for the coming ordeal. Steady, she told herself, clamping her jaw on chattering teeth. She was going to go through with this if it killed her.

To take her mind off what was coming, she looked around at the other members of the class. They were all girls, except for one pale little boy with flaxen hair who was sucking his thumb and looking reproachfully into space through luminous, tear-filled eyes. Obviously Maddy wasn't the only one suffering from the jitters. Several other children were clutching brightly colored towels like security blankets and trying to look brave. Only one child, a plump little girl with stubby black pigtails, actually seemed to be happy with the situation. She kept waving to her mother in the observation balcony, and receiving the requisite nods and waves in return. With that reassurance she strutted to the pool's edge, plunked herself down, and began energetically slapping the water with her feet. How Maddy envied her.

She just wished the instructor would hurry up! This suspense was awful. She wondered which one it would be—that nice, stocky young Oriental boy who had taken her registration card at the desk, or the girl with the long blond braid and the red, lifeguard's T-shirt over her bathing suit who was hosing down the far end of the deck.

And then suddenly she stopped speculating. Her heart took a sickening dive that landed it somewhere in the vicinity of her knees. Oh, Lord, she fervently prayed, please, *please* don't let it be *that* one. . . .

The man who had just come out of the office and had paused to talk to the Oriental lifeguard was wearing a T-shirt over his red, lifeguard's trunks too. A white shirt with the Parks and Rec logo on it. Below the trunks his legs were long and very muscular—swimmer's legs. And that T-shirt couldn't begin to hide the thickness of his neck and bicepses, or the width of his shoulders, or the depth of his chest, or the trimness of his waistline. The man was definitely a swimmer. World-class, if perfection of body was any indication. But that wasn't the only reason Maddy's knees had turned to jelly. He was carrying a clipboard, to which were clipped the familiar blue registration slips, and he kept turning his head to glance at the small, ragged assembly waiting on the pool deck. And now he was moving toward them with a frown corrugating his brow. God had obviously not seen fit to answer her prayers.

The man was absolutely gorgeous—or would have been if he hadn't been looking so stern and forbidding. His hair was brown—thick, wavy, and tousled, as if he'd climbed out of the water, combed it with uncaring fingers, and allowed it to dry that way. It was highlighted with the rusty gold that comes of almost constant exposure to sun and pool chemicals. His face was made rugged by a nose that had come in second best in at least one encounter with an immovable object, and a chin with a slightly off-center dimple. His forehead was wide and sunburned, his eyes close-set beneath sun-bleached brows. His mouth, though set in lines that looked harsh and hostile, was nicely shaped. And, for some reason, he seemed familiar. Although she couldn't imagine where or when, Maddy felt certain she'd seen him before. . . .

She suddenly became aware of furtive movements all around her. The children, awed and intimidated by the instructor's scowl, were gathering close to her, recognizing and moving instinctively toward the closest thing to maternal protection available. Something touched Maddy's leg, tickling. One child, a frail little dark-haired girl, had edged so close that the sleeve of the T-shirt the child wore over her bathing suit was brushing Maddy's leg.

Without thinking, Maddy dropped her hand to the thin, bony shoulder. With a quick, fearful movement the child looked up, and Maddy found herself gazing into a pair of huge, apprehensive brown eyes. And for just a moment she forgot her own fears. That look— she'd seen it too many times before. She swallowed a lump in her throat and with a warm, reassuring smile, opened her hand. The girl's small brown one crept into it like a hunted animal seeking refuge.

"I'm sorry," the instructor said, stopping directly in front of Maddy. He sounded like an impatient and beleaguered man trying very hard to be polite. "If you must stay, you'll have to wait on the observation deck with the other mothers. But it really would be better—"

"I beg your pardon?" Maddy's voice emerged as a low and completely bewildered croak.

The man frowned at his clipboard. "No moms allowed in this class—sorry. The mothers-and-kids class meets in the mornings."

"But I'm not—"

"If there's a mistake, I'm sure the office can help you straighten it out. Maybe they can move her into a morning class." His gaze dropped to the child beside Maddy, and suddenly softened. "Or she can stay—see how it works out. . . ." He dropped to one knee. Balancing the clipboard on the other knee, he held out a large, tanned hand. The girl flinched, and shrank against Maddy's legs.

The man smiled. Without warning, Maddy felt a curious little squeezing sensation in her heart; at the same moment, she experienced another wave of *déjà vu.*

"Hey," the instructor said, "my name's Zack. What's yours?"

"Theresa," the child whispered. She stared warily at the offered hand, but didn't relinquish her death grip on Maddy's. After a moment's hesitation the man reached out and gave the tail of the little girl's T-shirt a friendly tug.

"You look pretty tough to me," he said. "I'll bet you could handle this class all by yourself. What do you say you let your mom go over there with the other moms while we give it a try?"

In a barely audible voice Theresa said, "She's not my mother."

"Sister?"

A solemn head-shake rejected that. The instructor glanced up at Maddy, who was beginning to wish passionately that the concrete deck would open up and swallow her. He did a double take, then let his gaze travel slowly upward, taking in every single inch of Maddy's body, lingering on the place where her breasts made generous hemispheres and the nipples still stood out in merciless relief under the sleek black suit.

"Baby-sitter?" he ventured, frowning again.

"No," Maddy said miserably, and cleared her throat. "I'm not—I'm . . . uh . . . I think I'm in this class. You should have my registration card there someplace. Maddy Gordon?" She faltered in the face of the man's silence. "I signed up last winter . . . spring. I'm sorry, nobody told me. I did put down my birth date—right there on the card—and no one said a thing. I'm sorry. I'll—"

"You're . . . a student?" That wonderful smile was only a rapidly fading memory. The eyes that had flamed for one moment were a dark, smoky blue. "Are you sure you're a beginner?"

"Oh, yes," Maddy said, laughing nervously. "Absolutely." There wasn't a glimmer of response. Oh, Lord, she thought, why couldn't it have been someone jolly and friendly, like that boy in the office, or someone who might understand, like the girl with the braid? Why, oh, *why* did she have the bad luck to get stuck with Aquaman?

And why did he look so familiar? It didn't seem likely she'd have met him in the course of her job. On the one side, all the men she knew were either district attorneys, public defenders, or social workers—earnest, harried individuals with permanent worry wrinkles and paunches. And on the other . . . Well, no, certainly not. It was true that the people she faced every day came from all levels of society, but most of them had the characteristics she'd learned to recognize, the unmistakable signs of underlying anger and tension. No, she would stake her professional reputation that, for all his powerful build and forbidding expression, this man had no capacity for violence.

Admittedly, she'd arrived at that conclusion by completely subjective and unscientific means. She'd watched his hands. She'd watched him when he stood up, noticing the way he'd first placed a calm, reassuring hand on Theresa's shoulder, as if he understood instinctively that a sudden, violent movement would frighten her.

"Okay," he said now, raising his voice and turning to the other children as if Maddy had ceased to exist. "First thing we're all going to do is . . . drop everything. Right. Drop it right down on the ground, just like this." The clipboard clattered to the deck. The thumb-sucker stared at him with round, startled eyes. The two with towels dropped them and giggled nervously. Theresa clutched a handful of her T-shirt and glanced up at Maddy.

"Next thing we're all going to do is this." Zack raised his arms above his head and placed one hand over the other. Four pairs of childish arms followed suit readily, while Theresa gave Maddy a questioning look.

"Go on," Maddy whispered, squeezing the damp little hand. "Try it." Another pair of arms went up. Maddy started to lift hers, too, and then, feeling indescribably foolish, lowered them and cleared her throat. "Mr. . . . Zack—"

"Okay," the instructor said, ignoring the interruption, "now we're all ready to dive right into the pool! Ready, set—"

Five pairs of eyes got big and round. One by one the arms came down. The thumb-sucker looked ready to cry again, and even the plump, happy girl looked uncertainly at that huge, empty expanse of water.

"Smart kids," Zack said solemnly, nodding his head. "You guys are absolutely right. You know you aren't ready to jump into the pool, don't you?" Five little heads moved slowly back and forth. "Okay, I want you to remember that. Rule number one is: Nobody gets into the water unless I, or one of the other lifeguards, is right here. Got it? Great. My name's Zack. Nice and easy. Now your turn. Your name is . . ."

As he pointed a finger at each child, a name would pop out, accompanied by the giggles, hops, and fidgets of suppressed energy. Zack's stern, no-nonsense manner didn't seem to daunt the children a bit, now that they'd gotten used to it. Even Theresa hadn't felt the need to reclaim Maddy's hand, and had moved timidly forward to join the others.

But it sure daunted Maddy. "Zack," she said hoarsely, trying again to get his attention.

"Yes?" His glance was determinedly polite, but somehow didn't quite connect with her. It kept sliding off her left shoulder and hitting somewhere in the empty middle distance.

Maddy was beginning to feel trickles of anger seeping in around the mental blocks of fear and embarrassment. Struggling valiantly to remain calm and reasonable, she asked, "What would you like me to do?"

His response was unexpectedly disarming—a smile that tugged at his mouth and managed to pull it attractively awry. "Why don't you stay for today? Might even learn something." His gaze moved as if beyond his control, sliding over her body and resting briefly on the golden waves of her hair. It was like a physical touch, and throughout her body her nerve endings shivered and contracted in response.

Then suddenly, almost as if he'd called it ruthlessly to heel, his gaze left her and the smile disappeared. His voice became cold and impersonal. "After this, we'll see if we can find you an adult class. Now," he said briskly, retrieving the children's attention, "everybody over here. I want you to sit right down here on the edge of the pool."

With one graceful motion he took off his shirt and jumped into the water. The muscles of his chest and torso jerked and rippled as he walked backward in the waist-deep water, skimming the water's surface with his hands. Maddy closed her eyes. It was a beautiful chest, and his hands looked almost as if they were caressing the water, but right now she couldn't really appreciate such things. She felt slightly seasick. Her throat was dry and her heart was pounding. Moving as if her head might fall off if she tilted it, she sat down and lowered her feet into the tepid water.

Something touched her thigh like a small wet kiss.

"It's all right," Theresa said solemnly. She gave Maddy an unblinking, unsmiling stare, then turned resolutely back toward Zack. "*I'm* not afraid. Are you?"

Maddy lied. "Nope." Her chest had suddenly grown too small for her heart. She lifted her chin, sniffing a little as she smiled down at the shiny black head. "I'm not if you're not."

"Okay," Zack said, "now I want you all to turn over—tummies down, that's it—and let yourselves into the water, nice and easy."

Maddy looked desperately at Zack, begging silently for an exemption. She only got a hard, commanding stare in return. She hesitated a moment longer, considering rebellion, but Theresa was watching her, waiting for her. Her whole body, and particularly her vulnerable backside, burned with embarrassment, but Maddy followed instructions.

"See?" Zack said approvingly. "That's the way I want you to get into the pool, at least until you've learned to jump in. Now, you're standing on a platform. That's so the water only comes to your waist. If you get off the platform, the water's going to come up to your nose. So rule number two is: Don't get off the platform. Okay?" There was a moment's silence while he studied the water lapping around Maddy's knees. "Except for you, Maddy. You can get off the platform." The gently teasing tone surprised her. So did the glint of humor in his eyes.

Feeling confused, but a little less ridiculous, Maddy stepped down off the platform. She folded her arms resolutely across her waist and clamped her teeth together, doing her best to control her shivers.

The plump, pigtailed girl, whose name was Jennifer, bounced merrily off the end of the platform. Without comment, Zack extended an arm to retrieve her.

"Okay, when I count to three, I want everybody to turn around and put one hand on the wall—got that? One hand. One . . . two . . . *three*. Okay, great. Rule number three is: You have to keep one hand on the wall all the time, unless I tell you to let go."

Dear Lord, Maddy thought. How had she gotten herself into this nightmare? *Please, Lord, just let me get out of here. . . .*

Everybody know how to hold your breath?" Zack asked. "Sure, you do. Just like this, see?" There was a chorus of giggles. Maddy opened her eyes to the incredible specter of Zack, with eyes crossed and cheeks puffed out like a blowfish, slowly turning purple. The children were all doing their best to imitate him.

"Come *on*," Theresa whispered earnestly. "You have to hold your breath. If you don't, you'll get *drownded*."

Maddy took a deep breath and held it, painfully

conscious of the way her expanded lungs pushed her breasts against the tight black skin of her suit.

"Uh-uh," Theresa said firmly. "Like *this*."

Maddy dutifully puffed out her cheeks, then looked up just in time to catch Zack watching her with a quizzical expression on his face. Her pent-up breath escaped in a rush.

"Okay, I think we're ready for the big time," Zack said as he patiently hauled Jennifer back onto the platform. "That's right—we are going to put our faces in the water! I'm going to say, 'One, two, ready,' and you're going to take a big breath. Then I'm going to say, 'Go,' and I want you to put your face right down in the water. Okay? One . . . two . . . ready . . ."

Please, Lord, Maddy prayed. This is a good time for the Big One . . . the big California quake. . . .

"*Go.*"

Maddy leaned forward and stared down at the choppy surface of the water. Her neck and jaw muscles turned to concrete. She felt a wave of nausea, and thought desperately, *If I get sick now, I'll kill myself.*

Something touched her arm. Both arms. Near her ear a low, masculine voice rumbled, for her alone, "I won't force you to put your face down. I won't push you. You have to do it by yourself. Understand?"

She nodded, refusing to look at him.

"You can do it," the voice insisted. "I'm here for moral support, but *you can do it.*"

She nodded again. She knew only one thing for certain. If she didn't do it now, she never would, and all this humiliation would have been for nothing. Taking one more, excruciating breath, she closed her eyes tightly and plunged.

It was like jumping off a building. It seemed forever before she felt the clinging, suffocating wet close over her face, and longer than forever before she was out of it and breathing again, gasping and blowing and frantically brushing water from her face as if it were sticky nightmare cobwebs.

"Good job," Zack said quietly, and only when he released her did she realize he had been holding her all the time, supporting her with strong hands on her waist. She began to shiver.

"Now," Zack said to the rest of the class, "see how Maddy went all the way under the water and got her hair wet? That's what we're going to do next. This time when I say, 'Go,' I want you to bob down and get *all* your hair wet. Hey, not until I say, 'Go,' Jennifer. No dry hair allowed, got it? Okay . . ."

Maddy had been hearing Zack's voice through a funny, high-pitched ringing. She must have water in her ears, she thought fuzzily, just before somebody turned all the lights off.

Fortunately, Zack was standing so close to Maddy that he felt her sway and go slack, and was easily able to catch her before she slipped under. Then he was really in a hell of a predicament—arms full of a beautiful, unconscious blond, and five pairs of baby owl eyes focused on him with varying degrees of alarm. Okay, Zachary, he thought. Let's see you get out of this one.

But for the moment, heaven help him, he wasn't even thinking about getting out of it. He was looking down at her still, pale face and seeing it flushed and warm instead, with the curve of her cheek just fitting his palm. Her lips were a deep, dusky rose, and even slack and parted, showing the glistening tips of even white teeth, they looked full, and sweet, and incredibly inviting. It was ironic, really, after all the time he'd spent fine-tuning his protective reflexes and shoring up his barricades, that someone should slip past his guard *here*, in a babies' swim class, of all places!

But, as he'd learned the hard way, life was full of surprises.

He'd wondered at first if she might be some sort of celebrity chaser, though it had been awhile since he'd had to deal with that sort of nuisance. But that idea hadn't lasted any longer than it had taken him to spot the fear in her eyes. Her eyes . . . just like that little kid's. He supposed that was why he'd thought they belonged together. They both had that same scared look.

"She gonna be okay?" a woman asked. It was Sherry, one of the on-duty lifeguards, leaning over the edge of the pool to peer with concern and interest at his burden.

Zack nodded. "Yeah. She fainted, but I think it's just a case of nerves." Panic, he thought, would be more like it.

"Swept her right off her feet, huh?" Sherry said, deadpan, then levered herself into the water, planting herself between Zack and the round-eyed children. "Hey, who told you guys you could let go of the wall? Let's see one hand on the wall, now, okay?" In an aside to Zack she muttered, "I'll take over here. Get her outa here before they start getting hysterical."

Zack nodded and turned to wade toward the steps. Thank heavens for Sherry, he thought. The girl was barely nineteen, but had a level head and a way with children.

A voice piped up. "Is she sick?" That would be Jennifer, of course, asking bluntly the question that had been in all of their eyes. Zack turned and opened his mouth to answer, but instead of Jennifer's plump face and bright, interested gaze, he found himself meeting a pair of eyes as round and dark and liquid as two cups of coffee.

"Nah," Sherry said briskly, making a squirt gun with her hands. "Just dizzy. Some people get dizzy when they stare at the water for a long time. It's called vertigo. Any of you guys feel dizzy? No? Great. So what are you doin' with dry faces? Let's all take a big breath and start *bobbing!*"

Zack grinned, shook his head, and started again for the steps. Damn, Maddy Gordon wasn't exactly a dainty little bundle. She was almost as tall as he was and . . . He glanced down, swallowed, and stared resolutely straight ahead. Healthy. Very healthy. And all that thin, wet black nylon did was make her look like she'd dipped that spectacular body in ink.

Zachary, you're an idiot, he told himself. This was obviously a woman with problems. And problems, heaven knows, he'd had enough of. With grim determination he divorced his libidinous mind from the warm, voluptuous body in his arms.

It wasn't as difficult as he'd thought it would be. The image that followed him out of the pool and into the office was of another face entirely. A pinched little face with scared brown saucer eyes that tore at his heart. What was her name, anyway? Oh, yeah. Theresa.

Maddy's first thought was: How strange. She was dry.

She opened her eyes and stared through a dark tunnel at a white moonscape, which turned into an acoustical ceiling as her field of vision slowly expanded.

She was lying down; how did she get to be lying down?

She heard the murmur of voices and lifted her head to find out where they were coming from. What she saw was Zack's back. He was standing a few feet away, talking in a low voice to the Oriental lifeguard and unconcernedly dripping pool water onto the floor. From some distance away came the sounds of splashing, and a girl yelling directions and encouragement in a voice like a drill sergeant's.

Maddy lay very still, frowning at that magnificent back as she took a quick mental inventory. She was dry because she'd been wrapped from toes to chin in a scratchy blanket. And she was lying on a canvas fold-ing cot. The acoustical ceiling belonged to the pool office. So far so good. But there could be only one explanation for all of this.

She groaned out loud. "Oh . . . damn. I bet I passed out, didn't I?"

"Cold," Zack said mildly, turning to look at her. She watched apprehensively as he walked toward her. "Feeling better now?"

She nodded, wondering if he was being sarcastic or was sincerely concerned for her well-being. Now she found herself gazing at his legs instead of his back, following trickles of water as they made their way over hills and hollows of muscle and through sparse for-ests of hair. He wasn't overly hairy. She liked that. And then, mortified as much by her thoughts as by her circumstances, she closed her eyes and moaned softly. "You didn't call anyone, I hope?" She had hor-rifying visions of wailing sirens and paramedics.

He shook his head and squatted beside her, balanc-ing on his heels. "You weren't out more than a minute. Only just long enough to scare the daylights out of my class."

"Oh, Lord. Poor little things. I'm sorry. I never thought this would happen." She opened her eyes, and winced when she encountered that dark, smoky look. If only he wouldn't keep frowning at her like that. She'd had all sorts of responses from handsome males, ranging from obnoxious come-ons to acute bashfulness. She'd never had one keep scowling at her as if she were an annoyance he didn't know what to do with.

"Don't you think you should have told me you had a problem?" he asked.

"Problem?" Maddy shifted her frown to his chest and found that view no more comfortable than the other. "There's nothing wrong with me, except that I can't swim."

"Like hell there isn't. Normal people don't keel over when they put their faces in the water!"

"Normal!" Bristling in automatic defense, Maddy raised herself on her elbows. "I'm not sick! There's nothing physically wrong with me!"

He made a choking noise and stared at the hands that he was clasping between his knees. "I can see that," he said, nodding solemnly.

Maddy looked down at herself and went incandescent with embarrassment. "I didn't mean—" she said, trying to achieve the illusion of shrinking. She glanced up, straight into a pair of eyes that were lighted now with that elusive spark of humor. The spark ignited and became a glow that sent warmth oozing right down through her insides.

And then he grinned.

The soft, oozy feeling inside her congealed, quick-frozen by a cold wave of shock. Because all of a sudden Maddy knew who he was.

Two

The grin had done it. Maddy might not have been a swimmer, but she'd had the same dreams and fantasies as other thirteen-year-olds, and for her entire eighth-grade year that grin, and a slightly slimmer, smoother version of that chest, had decorated the inside wall of the gym locker she'd shared with her best friend, Chris.

But that wasn't the only place she'd seen that grin. For a year or so it had sparkled at her from the cereal box at breakfast, and promoted sugar-free soft drinks on the billboards she rode her bicycle past on the way to school. And along with a glorious slow-motion sequence of his specialty—the butterfly stroke—that was pure poetry set to music, it had helped pitch the healthful properties of milk, on television at night.

"Zack . . ." she said on a long, drawn-out breath, knowing a kind of fatalistic dread. "You're Zachary London, aren't you?"

The grin faded slowly. Maddy was sorry to see it go. It had been like a brief reunion with a long-lost friend.

Zack nodded, and without taking his gaze from her face said simply, "Yeah."

"Oh, no," Maddy said dismally, and covered her eyes with her arm. "Why me? All I wanted to do was learn to swim. *Anybody* could teach me to swim. A high school kid. A Boy Scout."

"I doubt that," Zack said dryly.

Anger began to melt the prickly ice of shock. "And who do I get for a teacher? Zachary London. *Zack London!* Five Olympic gold medals and three world records—or was it the other way around?" It didn't occur to her until later that she was being inexcusably rude. She was frustrated and shaken and definitely not thinking clearly. She sat up suddenly, glaring. "Do you have any idea how humiliating it is to be a grown-up person living in Southern California and not know how to swim? And how long it took me to get up the courage to do something about it?"

"I think I do," he murmured softly, but she ignored him.

"Do you know how embarrassing it is to find out you're in the wrong class? And then—" She threw up her hands dramatically. "Zack London. I can't believe it. I just can't believe it."

Throughout this tirade Zack sat on the floor with his arms draped over his drawn-up knees, watching her quizzically and patiently, waiting for her to run down. When she seemed to have run out of steam he slowly shook his head and muttered sardonically, "Well, I've gotten some pretty interesting reactions from women before, but yours is certainly unique."

"Why?" Maddy asked suddenly, getting her second wind. "Why do you do this, anyway? Teach beginners. In a place like this. It's like . . . it's like—" She waved her arm angrily. "Like hiring Mickey Mantle to coach T-ball!"

Zack suddenly burst out laughing. When Maddy went on glaring at him he used a hand to remold his features into somber lines and said in a strangled voice, "I'm sorry you're upset. I really am. And I'm not laughing at you. It's just—" He cleared his throat, looked away from her while he appeared to collect himself, then looked back. His face was straight and under control, but the glint of humor remained. "In answer to your question—I don't usually teach the beginners. I'm just standing in for the high-school kids and Boy Scouts until school's out next week."

"Oh," Maddy murmured. Something was happening to her as a result of that prolonged eye contact. She couldn't seem to remember how to breathe.

"I do coach the swim team and teach lifesaving, though. And I have a question for you, Maddy Gordon."

She blinked at him, suddenly apprehensive.

"How *did* you get to be an adult person in Southern California without learning to swim?"

"Haven't lived in Southern California that long. I'm a transplant from the Midwest—Indiana." She shivered and hunched her shoulders, wishing for a towel or a wrap of some kind.

She'd forgotten about the blanket. Zack leaned forward and drew it up around her shoulders. The movement brought his face close to hers. "Indiana has a terrific public swim program," he said. "You haven't answered my question."

The sensation produced by the warm stirring of his breath on her skin was indescribable. She shivered again, and he tugged the blanket together across her breasts.

"So . . . how come you never learned to swim?"

"No big deal," she mumbled. "I'm just afraid of water."

"Why?"

She shrugged. "I don't know. I just always have been."

"Baloney. Nobody's born afraid of water. We spend the first nine months of our lives happily immersed in it. What happened to make you afraid?"

She pushed back a strand of wet hair and said lightly, "Who knows? Maybe I had a bad experience when I was little. Maybe I almost drowned or something. I really don't remember." He knew she was lying; she could see it in his eyes. But she returned his disbelieving stare with stubborn defiance, letting him know that she'd gone as far as she was going to go.

"Well," he said, recognizing a brick wall when he saw one, "it would help if you could remember. It does a lot of good just to talk about things like that, you know."

Maddy bit her lower lip, but remained silent. Oh, she knew that—how well she knew that. But she wasn't the sort of person who went around blurting out her deepest feelings to strangers. Especially a stranger who just happened to have been an international celebrity and the object of her adolescent dreams!

Zack took a deep breath and stood up, acknowledging defeat. "Okay," he said briskly. "Let's see if we can find you an adult class. I'm sure you won't have so much trouble if you've got the company of others in the same boat."

He walked to the desk and began shuffling through papers, looking for a schedule. Maddy found that she could breathe again without having to think about it, but now she felt strangely off kilter, as if someone had removed some of the supports that kept her balanced and perpendicular to the ground. She seemed to be leaning in the direction he had gone, as if pulled by an invisible magnetic force.

"That's funny," he was saying, frowning down at the schedule in his hands. "There doesn't seem to be an adult-beginners' class this session. Guess there wasn't enough demand for one. Okay, that takes care of that." He dropped the papers back onto the desk and leaned against it, folding his arms across his chest. The stance made him look even more like a comic-book superhero. "Have you considered private lessons?"

"I hadn't," she said, focusing doggedly on the off-center dimple in his chin. "I wouldn't even know whom to ask. Look—" She stood up abruptly, gathering the blanket around her. "I've taken up enough of your time. You have a class to teach, and I've already upset the children, and anyway, it's not that important. I can learn to swim any time. Maybe next time they decide to offer an adult-beginners' class . . ."

She was moving past him, making for the women's shower room, trailing the blanket behind her like a queen's robes. Zack planted one foot firmly on the end of the blanket and said, "Whoa."

It was either stop or make her exit in nothing but her bathing suit. Maddy stopped.

"It's important," he said. "It was important enough that you signed up for lessons and showed up for the class. You said that took courage, and I believe you. It was important enough that you stuck it out when you found yourself in a class full of babies, and important enough that you put your face in the water even though you were scared to death to do it. So what's changed? Not a damn thing. You know what I think? I think you *need* to learn to swim." He tapped his head. "Psychologically. Not just because it might save your own life or somebody else's someday. Right?"

She stared resentfully at him and didn't answer. Who did he think he was, anyway, a psychologist or something? And why was he so determined to make a crusade out of her inability to swim? Why should he care? She would have thought that after the mess she'd made of his swimming class he'd be more than glad to be rid of her. And she couldn't understand the way he was looking at her, with his brows drawn together and his eyes that smoke color she found so unsettling.

"Well, look," he said abruptly, as if he'd just come to the same conclusion she had about wanting her out of his hair. He turned to scribble on a message pad. "Here's a couple of phone numbers. These are life-guards here at the pool who give private lessons during the summer. Right now they're still in school, but as soon as school's out they'll be available during off hours. Why don't you give one of these guys a call? They'll be glad to take you on, and I think they'd be pretty reasonable, too." He strolled toward her and tucked the paper inside the overlapping edge of the blanket. "And," he added, his voice unexpectedly gentle. "Promise me you'll do it, okay? It really is important." He smiled at her, the same warm, reassuring smile he'd used to break the ice with Theresa.

Theresa, Maddy thought. She'd almost forgotten. There was something she needed to tell him about Theresa.

With a sizable effort she pulled herself together, took a deep breath, and said, "Okay, I'll look into it. I promise. Zack . . . um . . ." She cleared her throat and focused on him, steeling herself against the distraction of his charisma. If anything was important, this was. "I think there's something you should be aware of. It's about that little girl—the one you thought—"

"Theresa." He was suddenly alert. "Yes, what about her?"

She hesitated. It wasn't as difficult to talk to him now that she was on familiar footing—her home territory, so to speak—but this kind of thing was never easy. "I'd like to ask you a question," she said carefully.

"Shoot."

"Why did you let Theresa wear her T-shirt in the pool? The pool rules state specifically, 'No T-shirts or cut-offs.' "

Zack's eyes narrowed slightly. "I noticed the way she was hanging on to it, and it didn't seem like a good time to make an issue of it. Why?"

"Because I think there's at least a possibility she

may have had a good reason for wanting to keep it on."

"I see." He straightened, looking thoughtful. "Marks, you mean. Something she's embarrassed about."

"More likely afraid," Maddy said, lowering her voice. "I may be wrong. I hope so. But . . . there are signs. Certain things you learn to look for."

He was silent for a moment, looking gravely at her. "You sound like you know what you're talking about," he said finally. "Are you a psychologist, or a cop?"

"No, but I often work with both. I work for a county social-services agency called the Family Crisis Center." She took a deep breath. "I work with abused children."

"Oh, boy." Zack exhaled slowly and rubbed a hand over his face. "Okay. So what do you want me to do?"

It warmed her, that unquestioning acceptance. Nearly everything about him either warmed her or unnerved her. "Just keep an eye on her. And if you do notice anything . . . suggestive, please give me a call, okay?"

Except for his nod he was very still. "All right. I'll do that."

She murmured, "Thanks," and after a moment's hesitation, turned to continue on her way to the showers. Halfway there she looked back. He hadn't moved a muscle, but was still watching her with eyes that were dark and unreadable, like smoke.

Maddy was still thinking about those odd, enigmatic eyes as she drove down the dark, leafy tunnel of avocado trees to her house. Her house was what the rental agent had called "a rare find." It was in the part of town known as the Heights, a hilly area that had retained most of its rural character in spite of the fact that its avocado orchards and citrus groves had been converted to well-designed and marginally expensive housing tracts. Still, a few small groves remained, and some of the homes were the original ranch houses or converted outbuildings, where people kept goats and chickens and indulged eccentricities that wouldn't have been tolerated in the city's limits.

Maddy's house had been a storage barn for farm machinery, which someone had turned into a guesthouse, or maybe a studio. It had no windows, except for one over the sink in the tiny afterthought of a kitchen. Sunshine poured like gold dust through five skylights that could be raised and lowered with ropes, letting in fresh air. At night Maddy could lie in bed and look up at the stars.

As she let herself in the front door, a huge blue Persian cat seemed to grow out of a shelf above the sofa, extending first horizontally, then vertically, and then in several directions at once. His stretch completed, the cat dropped disdainfully to the back of the sofa, then to the seat cushions, and finally to the floor. Carrying his tail aloft like a potentate's plumes, he paced regally toward the kitchen.

Maddy, watching him go, muttered fondly, "Incorrigible cat," and shook her head as she dropped her keys beside her answering machine. She flipped the switch to rewind the message tape and, settling herself on the arm of a chair, slipped her hand into the body of a fat pink dragon.

"Hi, Bosley," she murmured as the dragon's triangular head rose before her, mounted on a slender, blue-ridged neck. "Anybody call?"

The dragon stared at her with quizzical green eyes, wrinkled its nose, and croaked, "Don't try to wiggle out of it by changing the subject. You really made a fool of yourself today, didn't you?"

"I'd really rather not talk about it, thank you," Maddy retorted briskly, and plunked the dragon back on its stand as the message machine beeped and clicked. With its head askew, the dragon seemed to be listening to the recording along with her.

". . . Hello . . . Maddy? Um . . . I just called to see if you're free for lunch, but . . . um . . . I guess you aren't, are you? So . . . um. Okay, well, just call when you get a chance. 'Bye."

Maddy smiled. That was her best friend, Jody. She hated talking to the answering machine.

The machine beeped imperiously, signaling another message.

". . . Maddy—Larry here. I hate to do this to you, but we need you. Can you meet me at Juvenile Hall at . . . make it two o'clock? And bring your puppets, honey—it looks like a bad one. Deputies went in on a domestic-disturbance call. Found three kids in a locked room—you know the scene. Couple mattresses on the floor, nothing else but filth. Kids won't—or can't—talk. Sorry, babe . . . It's a lousy world. . . ."

There was a sustained beep and then silence. Both Bosley, the dragon, and Maddy, its creator, slumped disconsolately, staring at the answering machine.

"Well, I don't believe *that*," Maddy said firmly as she rewound the tape and reset the machine. She picked up the puppet, which immediately took on life and personality. It nudged Maddy under the chin, then peered at her with sad eyes. "Neither do I," it croaked staunchly.

"Boz," Maddy said in her own voice, smiling at the dragon, "it just can't be a lousy world when someone like me gets to meet Aquaman!" She stood up, supporting the puppet's pear-shaped body and long tail with her free arm. "But enough of fantasy—we have to go to work. Are you up to a real heartbreaker, Boz?"

"Have I ever failed you?" the dragon asked gently as Maddy gave its head a soulful tilt.

"Never," she answered as she carefully hung the dragon back on its stand. "Good old Bosley." She gave the dragon's blue-crested pink head an affectionate pat and went into the kitchen.

Three

"Amanda, you have *got* to tell me—what's he *like?*" Jody asked avidly when Maddy met her for lunch exactly a week later at their favorite deli.

"He's . . . *nice*," Maddy said, gazing at the salad bar as she bit absentmindedly into her meatball sandwich.

"*Nice?* Is that all you can say, *nice?* 'Nice' is the man who pumps my gas for me at the self-serve island. 'Nice' is the electricity meter man, who never, ever complains about the asparagus fern I have hanging right over the meter, even when it—"

"Almost," Maddy went on, inserting the words edgewise, "against his will."

"Amanda, my dear." Jody eyed her balefully. "You do realize that this is the man whom at one time, in my carefree youth, my entire dorm voted the man we'd most like to share a bathtub with? And now all you can think of to say about him is, 'He's nice'?" Jody sighed deeply. "How sad. That man had the most *gorgeous* body. Swimmers have such gorgeous bodies, don't you think? Swimmers and divers." She wriggled ecstatically. "And gymnasts. Lord, who could forget gymnasts? Gee, I love the Olympics, don't you?"

"He still does," Maddy said.

"Does what?"

"He still has that body."

"Wouldn't you know it." Jody stared accusingly at the last few bites of her submarine sandwich, then dropped it back onto her plate. "For some of us, twelve years makes a difference."

"Oh, it's made a difference in him too." Maddy frowned, sipping iced tea through a straw. "In other ways."

"Oh, yeah? How? What, exactly, does he look like? What have the years done to him? Is he bald? Wrinkled? Wouldn't surprise me—the sun does that to a person, you know. I tell that to myself every time I see one of those incredibly gorgeous tanned bodies that makes me feel like I just crawled out from under a rock! In ten years, I say to myself, you'll look like a map of Cleveland, and I—"

"It's not really physical," Maddy interrupted, laughing. "It's hard to explain. What's the first thing that comes to mind when you remember Zachary London? *Besides* that!"

"Hmm. I don't know." Jody considered. "His smile, I guess. He had that gorgeous—"

"Right. *The* smile. Every time you saw him being interviewed, even dripping wet and huffing and puffing, he'd be smiling. That smile just lit up his whole face."

"Well, he had a lot to smile about. All those gold medals, fame, a fortune from endorsements alone, a future in whatever branch of show biz he chose to bless—"

"You know," Maddy said softly, "I think it was the smile I always liked best about him."

Jody snorted. "Coming from you, Amanda, my dear, I'd almost believe that. So what about the smile? Oh, my God." She clamped a hand over her mouth. "He's lost his teeth!"

Maddy burst out laughing and choked on her iced tea. "His teeth . . . are *perfect*," she gasped out when she could speak again. "It's the smile he seems to have lost." She dabbed at her eyes and nose, sobering as she tried to figure out herself just what she meant by that statement. Because, of course, she *had* seen him smile—at her, and at Theresa. It was just . . . "He acts like he gave up smiling for Lent," she said, suddenly inspired. "Except that every now and then, one slips away from him, and he acts guilty. That's what I meant when I said he seems nice in spite of himself. He acts almost like he resents anyone who makes him smile."

"Oh, boy." Jody suddenly clapped both hands over her mouth, as if she were about to be sick. "I just remembered."

"What?"

"Oh, it's so awful." Jody transferred one hand to her eyes. "I know what happened to his smile. I don't know how I could have forgotten it for one minute. I can't believe it. Imagine him working with little kids . . . teaching swimming, of all things."

"Jody, what are you rambling about? Teaching swimming seems to me the most natural—"

"Don't you know what happened to Zachary London? It's been a few years ago now, but I don't know how you could have missed hearing something about it. It was such an *ironic* tragedy, you know?"

Maddy waited tensely as Jody leaned across the table and gripped her hand. "Maddy, he lost a child. His only child, I think it must have been—a little boy. He was about five years old."

Maddy felt as if someone had hit her in the stomach. "That's . . . terrible," she said inadequately. "How?"

Jody stared at her. "I can't believe you didn't hear about it. He drowned. A freak accident of some kind—

he'd been swimming since he was a baby, as you'd expect. Isn't that something? There he was, at the top of the heap. One of the world's blessed. Looks, fame, fantastic health, money, married that model . . . What was her name? They looked like Ken and Barbie. . . ."

For once Maddy was glad to let Jody talk. She was staring at nothing, imagining the unimaginable. The unspeakable.

"His wife?" she managed finally. The pain in her throat was awful. "It must have been terrible for her."

Jody frowned down at her plate. "I seem to remember something about her too. I guess it pretty much destroyed the marriage, though. It happens like that sometimes. I know Zachary just dropped out of sight. Gee, Maddy, I'm sorry. I sure rained all over our lunch, didn't I?"

"Oh, it's all right," Maddy said tightly. "I'm glad you told me. It explains a lot of things."

"Well, I could have picked a better time. We were having such fun. Anyway, you actually met Zack London. Hey, you know, I didn't even realize he lived in this town! Incredible." Jody sniffed, sounding vaguely put out. "Obviously," she said as they stood up to leave, "he can't have been living here very long."

Maddy laughed in spite of the ache that had stayed in her throat. It was probably true. Jody knew virtually everyone in San Ramon.

"So . . . do you think you'll ever see him again?" Jody asked.

Smiling wryly, Maddy shook her head. "I don't think so."

"Why not?" Jody sounded as wistful as a child denied a chance to meet Santa Claus.

But Maddy only smiled and gave Jody an enigmatic shrug. She didn't feel like trying to explain to her blithe and effusive friend that the only way she was likely to see Zack London again was if something happened that she hoped would never, never happen.

Fifteen minutes later she let herself into her house and made straight for the blinking message machine, scooping up Bosley on the way. She was feeling, not so much *depressed*, as . . . wistful.

"It's too bad," Jody had told her one day, "that you don't have a personality to match your looks."

"Well, your looks don't match your personality either," Maddy had pointed out.

"I know." Jody had sighed, gazing down sadly at her comfortably plump and rumpled self. "There is no justice. With your looks I could have either been a movie star or married a prince!"

"But Jody," Maddy had said, smiling, "you *did* marry a prince."

"Yes," Jody had agreed smugly, in that purring tone she acquired whenever she spoke of Mike. "I did, didn't I? Which just goes to show you—looks ain't everything!"

"No," Maddy said softly now to Bosley. "Looks sure don't ensure happiness, do they? Look at Zack . . ."

Look at me.

For once, the dragon had nothing to say. Maddy sighed and flipped the message button.

Moments later she was on her way back out the front door, and Bosley was draped haphazardly on his stand, swaying slightly in the breeze of her departure.

When Maddy drove into the parking lot of the San Ramon Municipal Park she wasn't sure what to expect. All Zack's message had said was, "Can you come to the pool before one-thirty? I think there's something you ought to see."

She couldn't understand what had made her heart jump like a startled rabbit at the sound of his voice on her answering machine, but it had been racing as if a pack of hounds was in hot pursuit ever since. And now, as she sat in her car, staring at the glass front of the pool building, she felt almost afraid. She'd been scared the last time she'd sat here, too, but that had been different. That had been butterflies, the cold, sick dread she'd grown accustomed to over the years. Right now she felt hot and shaky and confused.

In the last few days, she realized, her emotions had been under almost constant bombardment. She was beginning to feel besieged. She knew that the kind of work she did required a certain degree of insulation in order to survive it. People who let themselves get emotionally involved tended to burn out pretty quickly. Maddy had always managed to keep herself at arm's length—literally. Her puppets were her buffer. Which was really ironic, she thought, when you stopped to consider it. The very tools she used to reach those terrified and withdrawn kids kept her from being reached by them.

But that was before Theresa. How had that kid managed to get under her defenses like that? All because she'd made the mistake of trying to tackle an old hang-up. It had turned out to be like nudging the first in a lineup of dominoes. Her fear had made her sensitive to the embarrassment of being in the wrong class, and fear and embarrassment had made her vulnerable. And in that state she'd allowed one small brown hand to reach out and touch her. Touch *her*— not Bosley, or one of the other puppets. And she hadn't been prepared for what happened to her heart when she first looked down into those big, lost eyes. . . .

And then, on top of that, to be confronted with Zack London, literally in the flesh! And to suffer the unspeakable indignity of passing out cold in his arms! She'd already arrived at the realization that it had to have been Zack who had carried her into the office that day, Zack who had wrapped her in a blanket and placed her on the cot. And after all that, knowing who he was now and what had happened to him . . . Well, it was no wonder she was feeling nervous and awkward. Anyone would. As for getting the shakes at the sound of his voice, of course it was because she'd immediately realized he could only be calling about Theresa.

Maddy pressed her forehead against the steering wheel and closed her eyes. Oh, how she'd prayed she was wrong about Theresa. But it couldn't be anything else. Zack wouldn't call her for any other reason. Unless—her heart gave a hopeful lurch—he'd found an adult swim class for her after all! Maybe that was it. Maybe—

She reached for the car-door handle, then stopped. Theresa had come out of the pool building. She looked incredibly tiny, standing there in her yellow bathing suit and sandals, holding a towel around her shoulders like a cape. So small and unprotected. Maddy's heart ached as she watched the little girl search the parking lot, then begin to descend the steps one at a time, her sandals making slapping sounds on the cement.

Maddy sat very still, hardly breathing, as the child came slowly toward her. For a few moments she thought Theresa had seen and recognized her and was coming over to say hello. When she heard a man's voice, rough and impatient, coming from the car right next to hers, she was so startled, she jumped and banged her crazy bone on the door handle.

"Hey, come on. Get a *move* on!"

Theresa looked up, and Maddy's body went cold. She felt like a great big exposed nerve. One side of the little girl's face was discolored from temple to jaw. Her lip was swollen and the outer part of the white of her eye was blood red.

Fighting the urge to jump out of the car and grab the child, Maddy shifted her gaze to the fragile little hands. She saw them grip the chrome door handle and struggle to open the heavy door, then appear again on the windowsill as they tugged the door shut. Maddy caught one brief glimpse of a swarthy face, dark, curly hair, and a moustache. Then the car roared away.

And still Maddy sat, unable to move.

"You saw?" a voice asked. Zack was leaning over, looking at her through her open window.

She nodded, still staring straight ahead. "It's . . . different," she said in a low voice, "when you . . . when you . . ."

"When you're personally involved. Yeah, I can imagine." He put his hands on the windowsill, then reached for the handle and pulled the door open.

Maddy jerked her head sideways but still didn't look at him. "How do you know?"

His voice was grim. "I have a very vivid imagination. And I haven't done much else since you told me what you do, dammit, except imagine it. Come on. Let's go inside and talk about this. I'll get you a drink of water."

Maddy finally looked at him and felt a wave of shame. At least she'd had experience with this kind of thing. She'd had some warning, some preparation. Zack hadn't. His face looked like bleached bone.

Without a word she nodded and got stiffly out of the car.

As Zack followed Maddy into the pool office he was experiencing a particularly frustrating and futile kind of rage. It was a feeling he'd only had once before in his life.

"How do you take that, day in and day out?" He threw the question at her angrily, almost as an accusation. He found himself resenting her ability to "take it." Dammit, it seemed almost a kind of complicity. And it only enraged him further that she just looked at him with compassion in response to his rudeness, as if she understood how badly he needed to hit out at someone—anyone.

"I'll make this report, if you like," she said in a low voice. "Your name doesn't even have to be on it."

He stared at her. "What the hell do you mean? I

want my name on it! I'd like to personally strangle
with my bare hands whoever did that!"

"You'd be surprised how many people either don't
want to get involved at all or want the protection of
anonymity." She'd reached the telephone ahead of
him. She grabbed the receiver and held it in what
looked like protective custody while she met his furious stare. "I know who to talk to," she told him gently, and began to dial. Zack expelled a frustrated
breath and combed his hair back with his fingers.

"Family Crisis Center—Dr. Larry Whitlaw, please,"
Maddy said into the phone, still watching him with a
worried frown.

Zack took two agitated paces to the left, four back
to the right, and then, muttering under his breath,
pivoted and stalked into the men's dressing rooms.
He took his time showering and dressing, and even
wasted some more time trying to instill discipline in
his hair. That effort failed, but in the process some of
the discipline must have managed to penetrate to his
brain. He was calm when he went back out into the
office.

She was sitting on the corner of his desk, waiting
for him. She was wearing a white sundress with a full
skirt, and her long legs were crossed at the knee. She
looked like the original snow queen. Incredible, he
thought. The other day she'd been Marilyn at her
sexiest and most vulnerable; today she was Grace
Kelly. Who the hell was she really? And why did he
want to know?

"What happens now?" he asked harshly, jamming
his hands into his pockets.

Maddy took a deep breath. "The home environment
will be thoroughly checked out. Counseling and other
assistance services will be made available to the
family—"

"*Family!*" she sounded as if she were reading an
information booklet aloud! "What about that poor lit-

tle kid? Won't they get her out of there? Lock up whoever did that to her?"

"They may remove her from the home temporarily,
if the situation warrants," Maddy said carefully. "But
permanent separation is usually a last resort."

"Last resort? Whose?" He wanted to grab her and
shake her out of that maddening professional calm.
"What, does someday have to get killed first?"

"Zack." Her voice was very low and unusually
hoarse. She had to clear her throat before she could
go on. "These children love their parents, in spite of
. . . everything. Breaking up a home is . . . well, it's
very traumatic for the child. We try to help, not make
things worse."

Zack took a deep breath, held it while he glared
helplessly at the ceiling, then released it in a long
sigh. "I'm sorry. I just feel so . . . so damn . . ."

She stood up and laid a hand on his arm. "You did
the right thing. The right people are moving on it
now. Something will be done, I promise you."

But would it be the *right* thing? he wondered. And
would it be enough? He took another deep breath,
then realized his chest was aching in a way it hadn't
in a very long time. He stared down at the hand on his
arm, and she snatched it away. He reached out and
caught it. "Hey, listen, are you doing anything right
this minute?"

She'd made a startled little gasp when he'd grabbed
her hand, and was staring at him as if she thought he
might explode. "N-now?"

"Yeah. How about a cup of coffee or something? I
don't know about you, but I need to get out of here. I'd
like to talk about this a little more." He hesitated,
then added, "Preferably someplace quiet."

She was biting her lip, looking more like Marilyn
now than Grace. After a moment she said, "Okay.
How about my place?"

It was unexpected, to say the least, but he didn't

show how startled he was. He stood up and said crisply, "Your place it is. I'll follow you."

As he drove behind her nondescript white sedan down a long, creepy lane completely overhung with avocado trees, it occurred to him to wonder, and not for the first time, just what kind of woman he was dealing with. The trouble was, she gave off contradictory signals. She looked like a showgirl. That was the only way to put it. She was leggy and statuesque and blond, the kind of blond whom gentlemen are said to prefer. And what was she? A social worker, for Pete's sake! A social worker who dealt with mistreated kids. Zack still had trouble believing it. It had him feeling strangely out-of-step. It would be interesting to see her place. Maybe there he'd find the clues that would help him fit her pieces together.

And then he wondered again why it mattered. He felt guilty for thinking about her, when he should have been thinking about that little girl. But dammit, Theresa was there all the time anyway, in the back of his mind, and had been for days. And now it was out of his hands. He'd done what he could, and the rest was up to the people who knew how to deal with that kind of sickness. He had to get the kid out of his mind. Forget her. He had a feeling Maddy Gordon could help him forget.

It was quiet in the grove. He could hear the rustle of dry leaves under his tires, the call of a crow somewhere in the treetops. Ahead, fingers of sunlight slanted through openings in the trees, spotlighting an oddly-shaped weathered gray building with no windows. It looked like an enchanted cottage, isolated in a sunlit glade in the middle of a dark and mysterious forest. He kept expecting an ugly little old lady to come around the corner croaking, "Nibble, nibble like a mouse, who's been nibbling at my house?" Or seven fat little men to come marching down the lane singing, "Hi ho, hi ho, it's home from work we go!"

But when Maddy unlocked the front door and stood

aside to invite him inside the cottage, he realized he'd had the wrong story. "My Lord," he breathed after a moment's stunned silence. "It's Geppetto's workshop!"

From every shelf and chair and tabletop, faces peered at him; purple faces, blue faces, green faces, bright orange and yellow faces; faces with big sad eyes, faces with bright shoe-button eyes, faces with sleeping eyes, long curling lashes lying against fuzzy cheeks; animal faces, people faces, and faces born of pure imagination; faces with ears, faces with horns, faces with tufts and billows of iridescent hair. Each face was attached to a body, and most of the bodies had arms. But except for the ones suspended by wires from the ceiling, very few of the bodies had legs.

"Puppets," he said in wonder. "They're all . . . puppets." And then, with horrified disbelief, "My Lord— one's *alive!*"

For in one particularly furry, gray-blue face a pair of round green eyes had, unmistakably and oh, so slowly, *blinked.*

Maddy gave a delighted gurgle of laughter. "Incorrigible, you rascal, can the act and come down from there."

The green eyes closed and a pink mouth opened in a wide, insolent feline yawn.

Geez, Zack thought, is she a witch? It was becoming a matter of pride with him to appear unflappable around her, not to let her see how much she could surprise him. And so, to cover his shock and give himself a few seconds to regain his poise, he reached out and gathered up the big gray cat from his perch on a shelf full of puppets. The cat seemed momentarily nonplussed. It reared back its head to stare at him, then flattened its ears and squinted and sniffed at Zack's chin. And finally the cat went completely boneless in his arms, paws in the air, and began to purr.

"That was a test, you know," Maddy said. She was standing beside a small table that held a phone and message machine. It seemed to be the only surface in the place that wasn't covered with puppets or puppet parts.

Zack lifted one eyebrow. "Do I pass?"

"Oh, with flying colors. You're the first, I think." She smiled wryly. "Most people tend to . . . freak out, as a friend of mine would say, when Corry goes into his act."

"His *act*?"

"Corry likes to impersonate a puppet, and then frighten people out of their wits by coming to life. He's a born showman, and has faultless timing. He only does it for first-time visitors, and always when they're still in shock just from seeing the place. After that, I guess he figures they've got his number."

"Amazing," Zack murmured, and set the cat on the floor, much to its disgust. After a perfunctory wash designed to save face, Corry made his proud, unhurried exit.

"Yes, I guess he is," Maddy said, smiling fondly after the waving plume of tail.

"I wasn't talking about him." Zack gestured at the puppets and the magical stairways of sunlight that angled down from five skylights, then walked toward her. "I mean all of it. This house, the puppets . . . you."

"Me?" She shook her head emphatically. "I'm not amazing." Her voice shook, and her eyes seemed to darken. He realized with another shock that she was afraid of him. He felt the desire he'd first felt the day she'd fainted in his arms in the pool, the desire to erase that fear from her eyes. To see her eyes grow luminous and soft, and finally close in complete trust and surrender . . .

Very slowly, he reached out and touched the nose of the large pink dragon she had gathered into her arms. To his astonishment, the dragon sneezed, then rubbed its nose with its tail.

"Gesundheit," Maddy said, watching Zack over the

dragon's blue crest. She was smiling, her lips slightly parted, and her eyes held shimmers of laughter. "This is Bosley. Bosley, say hello to Zack."

The dragon muttered, "Hello." It sounded like a sulky frog.

"Bosley's nose is very ticklish," Maddy explained. "However, he does enjoy having his neck rubbed."

"Oh, yeah?" Zack murmured, and wondered if *Maddy* did. Feeling only a little silly, he stroked the velvet underside of the dragon's chin. The dragon made a purring sound. Zack was captivated and amused to see that its eyes had closed.

"My goodness," Maddy said, her voice sounding something like a purr as well. "I see you have a way with dragons as well as with cats and children. You must have a magic touch."

Zack didn't answer. He just looked into her eyes and slowly and with deliberate sensuousness began to stroke the dragon's neck. The dragon made delighted Mae West noises and wound itself around Zack's forearm. It rubbed its cheek ecstatically against his biceps, then rested its head on his shoulder and gazed up at him with adoring eyes.

"Hello, big fella," the dragon said in Mae West's sexiest voice.

Maddy looked startled. "Boz! You never told me you were a girl!" Her cheeks were as pink as the dragon.

"Honey," Bosley purred, "you never asked."

"You're good," Zack said softly to Maddy. "You're very, very good."

"Maybe," the dragon said, lowering her eyelashes demurely. But when I'm bad . . . I'm *better*."

"Boz!" Maddy seemed genuinely scandalized.

Zack laughed appreciatively, but even as he was doing so, he was battling intense frustration. She *was* good with that thing—too damn good. He knew exactly what she'd done, and knew that she'd done it deliberately. She'd used that puppet to hold him off, just as effectively as if it had been a third person—a roommate, say—instead of a toy made of velvet and papier-mâché.

But Zack hadn't forgotten for one moment that under the pink fabric and paint he had caressed a soft, shapely arm. And that the dragon's head, however uncannily lifelike Maddy's skill could make it seem, was a hand—Maddy's hand. And for a few moments it had stroked his arm and shoulder and rested warmly in the hollow of his neck. His skin still tingled with his awareness of her. It was a kind of awareness he hadn't felt in a long time—hadn't even wanted to feel. And right now he knew that he wanted her hands touching his skin without the interference of cloth and cardboard. In fact, he wanted her *skin* touching his skin, without interference from anything at all. . . .

But for the life of him, he didn't know how to get past her chaperones.

Four

Maddy saw that the smoky look was back in Zack's eyes and wondered if she'd gone too far. She couldn't imagine what had come over her, to use Bosley to flirt that way. Good heavens, a sensuous dragon! Who'd have thought she had it in her?

She didn't have it in her—not really. It was just the darn puppets. She was so accustomed to interacting through them in highly charged emotional situations that they sometimes took on personalities all their own. She glared accusingly at Bosley, but the dragon only returned her look of reproach with one of sleepy-eyed innocence. With a small noise of helpless dismay, Maddy plunked the puppet back onto its stand.

Now she felt naked and defenseless. Zack's presence in the huge, sunlit room made it seem too crowded, the air precious. Realizing that she was twisting her hands together in a childish manifestation of nervousness, she waved one in the general direction of the sofa and said, "Um . . . won't you sit down? I'll go fix some coffee—unless you'd prefer iced tea." She wondered for a moment if he needed something stronger after the shock of seeing Theresa, and was trying to remember whether she'd saved the bottle of rum Jody had brought to make eggnog last New Year's Day.

"Do you suppose," Zack asked with a disarming flash of his famous smile, "that I could have a glass of milk?"

A peculiar warmth flooded Maddy's chest. She found herself smiling back without her usual reserve. "Oh. You really *do* drink milk!"

His smile slipped. "Yeah . . . a habit that stayed with me." His hand was resting flat against his belly, just above the waistband of his jeans. Through the thin knit of his white polo shirt Maddy could see the sculptured muscles. She had a sudden vivid recollection of that chest, smooth and tan and beaded with water droplets, and felt an unfamiliar squeezing sensation in her own midsection.

Belatedly realizing that she'd been staring at both the hand and the body beneath it for quite some time in tongue-tied silence, Maddy felt the heat from her chest surge upward into her cheeks. She didn't know what she mumbled as she turned and made a hasty retreat to the kitchen.

Coward, she thought as she groped in a cupboard to find a glass. Idiot, she moaned inwardly as she opened the refrigerator and took out a carton of milk. What was the matter with her? He was only a man, and a very *nice* one, at that. Okay, so he was Zack London, but he wasn't Aquaman, or any other superhero. He was a perfectly ordinary, human man.

Except that there wasn't any way her brain was ever going to convince the rest of her that this man was "ordinary." Even now, as she watched him through her kitchen's pass-through window, she could feel the rhythms of her body change in subtle but frightening ways. Not only her pulse and respiration, but all her senses and life forces had somehow intensified. Even from this distance she could see the way the hair grew on the back of his neck, longish, unruly, undisciplined. And for the space of one heart-beat, like a dream or a memory in which a whole range of events and emotions are telescoped into a single instant of awareness, she knew what it would feel like to weave her fingers through the crisp silk of that hair and touch the hard-muscled column of his neck. She could feel his skin, like warm satin beneath her fingertips; she could smell it, soap and sunshine and a faint tang of chlorine; she could *taste* it. . . .

Amanda, for heaven's sake!

The sensual images collapsed under an avalanche of guilt. With a degree of care and concentration completely unwarranted by so simple a task, she poured a glass of milk and put the carton back in the refrigerator. Carrying the glass, and her body, like fragile crystal, she walked back into the cottage's main room.

Zack hadn't accepted Maddy's invitation to sit down. He was prowling the perimeters of the room, examining the puppets that filled and overflowed every shelf and tabletop.

"This is quite a hobby you have here," he said, turning as she moved toward him. Though his eyes were in shadow, making it impossible to see the expression in them, something about the stillness of his body as he watched her made her terribly self-conscious.

"Oh, well," she murmured with a little shrug as she handed him the glass of milk, "it's actually a bit more than a hobby."

His eyebrows lifted in surprise as he took the glass with an effortless grace Maddy envied. "Really? Are you a professional entertainer?"

"Professional, yes. Entertainer . . . . not exactly." Now her hands were empty again. To fill them, she picked up a little-girl puppet with round pink cheeks and a head full of bobbing, corkscrew curls. In a prominent place above one bright blue eye, there was a large Band-Aid. "This is Didi," Maddy explained as she settled the puppet, using her free hand to poke an errant curl into place. "She's one of the puppets I use most often in my work."

"Why does she have a Band-Aid?" Zack asked, smiling at Maddy as he touched it with a finger.

She gazed steadily at him and didn't return the smile. "That's the first thing the children always ask too," she said softly. "It's amazing what an icebreaker it can be."

"Icebreaker?"

"Yes. I use the puppets in my work with children like Theresa. Even very frightened and confused children will tell a puppet things they would never tell a strange adult."

Zack stared at her for a moment in tense silence. Then he muttered, *"God,"* under his breath and turned away from her to set his glass of milk, untasted, on the coffee table. Keeping his back to her and spacing his words with precision, he said, "What I don't understand is how you can deal with this kind of thing all the time. I guess you must just get . . . hardened, huh?"

"No," Maddy answered carefully. "Not hardened. You never get hardened. But insulated . . . maybe."

He turned back around. "You learn not to care, is that it?"

Wincing a little, but realizing that the anger in his voice wasn't really directed at her, Maddy spoke instead to the pain in his eyes. "Of course you care. But not . . . in a personal way." She fussed for a moment with the puppet, while she tried to think of a way to make him understand. "It's like a doctor," she said finally, touching the Band-Aid on the puppet's fuzzy brow. "Doctors care about their patients, but if they allowed themselves to become emotionally attached to them, they wouldn't be able to help them. They have to maintain a certain amount of distance— professional objectivity—in order to be effective. Do you understand? That's why doctors usually don't treat members of their own families."

Zack didn't answer immediately. Instead he picked up a puppet—a dog with sad eyes and long, floppy ears—and fitted it over his hand and arm. He cocked the puppet's head and opened its mouth in an experimental way. Then, to Maddy's surprise and delight, he reached out and touched Didi's cheek with its shiny black nose. "I'm sorry," he murmured as the dog gazed soulfully at Didi. "I had no right whatsoever to judge you like that."

Zack's dog puppet gave Maddy's Didi puppet a gentle nudge under the chin, but his eyes were looking across the two fuzzy heads and directly into Maddy's eyes. She opened her mouth, then closed it again in confusion. The sensation in her stomach was something like a stampede of butterflies. She couldn't think, let alone talk!

In a kind of panic she tore her gaze from those smoky eyes and gave Didi's curly yellow head a shake.

"Oh, that's okay, I understand," the puppet said in a sappy, little-girl voice. Manipulating the rod that operated Didi's right arm, Maddy made the puppet pat the dog's head. Then, in another one of those unexpected and dangerous impulses, Didi planted a quick puppet-kiss squarely on the dog's nose.

The dog gave a startled "Wuf!" and actually seemed to look taken aback. Maddy jerked her gaze back to Zack's face, once again afraid she'd gone too far. There was a peculiar little half-smile on his lips.

"I understand too," he said enigmatically, and, taking both his puppet and Maddy's, laid them carefully back on the shelf. Before she had any idea what he had in mind, he turned back to her, placed his hands on her shoulders, leaned across the space between them, and kissed her, oh, so gently, on the lips. And then again, softly, on the tip of her nose.

"I like it much better," he said firmly, "without go-betweens."

He released her, but she could still feel the weight of his strong hands on her shoulders, still feel the imprint of his mouth on hers. He moved away to finally, belatedly, take his seat on the couch. As he reached to pick up his milk glass, Corry appeared from nowhere. The cat bumped his head once against Zack's elbow, then arranged himself like a feather boa along and over one lean thigh.

For a moment Maddy and the cat just blinked at each other. "Yes . . . well, um . . ." Maddy cleared her throat and attempted an intelligent comment. Corry looked faintly disgusted. Maddy tried again. "I—" She gave up and sat down on the telephone table, a safe distance from the sofa.

Zack drank the milk and offered the glass to Corry, who haughtily sniffed it and declined. "Tell me what happens now," he said, frowning at the glass as he rolled it between his palms.

"To . . . Theresa?"

"Yes, of course." He lifted his gaze to hers, that funny half-smile back on his lips. "I'm pretty sure I know what's going to happen with *us.*"

Maddy's whole body broke into goose bumps, responding to something in his voice that felt strangely like warm hands on her skin. She looked desperately around for a puppet, but the only one within reach was Boz, and *she* certainly couldn't be trusted.

"Well," Maddy said, after clearing her throat once more, "first people—a juvenile officer and a public-health nurse, probably—will go pay the family a visit. They will check on the home environment, talk to the parents and tell them a report is being filed, check Theresa to see if she needs medical attention—" She stopped because Zack had made a noise, but he waved her on. She continued with more assurance, finding refuge from the unfamiliar feelings he was arousing in her, in the familiar realities of her professional routines.

"They'll evaluate the situation—recommend what needs to be done, put the parents in touch with the right agencies, support groups—"

"What about the kid?" Zack interrupted. "Won't they get her out of there? She's been hit before, I'd stake my life on it, and she's going to get hit again, unless somebody does something to stop it!"

"Somebody *is* doing something," Maddy said patiently. "You did the most important part—you reported it. Now let the professionals handle it. Zack . . . they do know what to do."

"Right . . . I know. I'm sorry." Controlling himself with a visible effort, he sat back and stretched his arms out along the top of the sofa. Maddy watched the thin knit of his polo shirt pull taut across his chest, and swallowed.

"Tell me something," he said, watching her with a thoughtful appraisal that made her self-consciousness even worse. "How did you get into this? Were you an abused child yourself?"

"Of course not!" She stared at him. "What on earth makes you think—"

He shrugged and said, "Sorry," but didn't soften his unnerving scrutiny. "It seemed to make sense. You have a pathological fear of water, and that kind of phobia usually comes from a real trauma of some kind, doesn't it? And then, you're unusually shy for such a beautiful woman—"

"I'm not!"

"Not shy, or not beautiful?" He was smiling at her now, a rare smile that touched his eyes with a soft sparkle.

Words failed her. Again. She felt gauche and stupid. She felt thirteen, with adolescent males staring, red-faced, at her bosom. What could she say that wouldn't sound either false or egotistical? She *was* shy, and she was supposedly beautiful. She'd been told often enough that she was. How could she ever hope to explain to anyone that she just didn't think of herself that way? On an unexpected tidal wave of memory came the image of her own nine-year-old face in the bathroom mirror, pale and round-eyed, trying not to wince as her mother's hands pulled and tugged her masses of corn-silk hair into tight, stiff braids. And above her own face was her mother's, thin-lipped with disapproval, her voice cold, her words punctuated by the jerking of her hands. "Pretty *is* as pretty *does*, Amanda. The devil himself can put on a pretty face."

Maddy took a deep breath and said evenly, "I'm not very good with snappy comebacks. And I'm not very comfortable with men who are self-assured and . . . glib."

"Glib?" He looked genuinely surprised. "That's the last thing I want to be. I'm just trying to get to know you better, that's all. I made an observation and came to a very natural conclusion. You certainly are beautiful, and you seem shy, at least around me."

"I guess maybe I am," she murmured, embarrassed by her churlishness. "Around you."

"Why?" He leaned forward suddenly, intent on her answer. When she only shrugged and muttered evasively, he prompted, "I don't make you nervous, do I? Why, because of the swimming? The fact that you fainted in my arms? What?"

Maddy stared at him, wondering if the man could possibly be real. "You're . . . Zack London!" To her, at least, that explained everything.

He made a disgusted noise and sat back, lacing his fingers behind his head. Corry gave a small meow of complaint and blinked in a resigned sort of way before rearranging himself on Zack's lap. After a moment Zack heaved a sigh, and said, "Maddy, I'm just a guy who worked real hard and practiced a lot, and that was a long time ago. Don't confuse me with some glossy image you saw on a billboard once upon a time. That wasn't me up there. I'm just a small-town guy. I'm nobody you should be intimidated by." He shook his head, and laughter crinkled the corners of his eyes for an instant. "If anything, I'd say you'd be accustomed to doing the intimidating."

Maddy found herself laughing, too, but with self-deprecation. "I guess I do intimidate some people, for some reason. I don't know why. Maybe because I'm so tall."

"Or so blond," Zack said with a straight face.

"But that isn't me either," she said earnestly. She touched her chest. "In here, I'm just . . . Amanda from Indiana." She shrugged helplessly, wondering if he would understand.

For a minute she thought he wouldn't. Then, to Corry's disgust, he stoood up and held out his hand. "Hello, Amanda from Indiana," he said briskly. "I'm Zachary. Nice to meet you."

Startled, and then entranced, Maddy slowly stood and placed her hand in his and felt its warmth flow through her. She heard herself say, "Nice to meet you, Zachary."

He didn't let go of her hand. "Overs?" he asked softly.

"Overs." Her own voice was breathy, and very faint.

"Good. Now, tell me, Amanda from Indiana, just what do you do?"

"I'm a social worker," she answered promptly, getting into the spirit of the thing. "Oh—and I make puppets."

"Great! We have a lot in common. I sell sporting goods. And I teach swimming."

She smiled, and felt the smile blossom into laughter. It felt good. "How nice! Children or adults?"

"Children." His eyes caught hers and held on. "And in rare and very special cases . . . adults."

She stared back at him, her smile fading, hopelessly tongue-tied once more.

"Maddy, I'd like to teach you to swim."

"Oh, no—I couldn't." She pulled her hand from his warm and oddly comforting grasp, and, because her hands felt so empty, picked up Bosley. Instead of fitting the dragon over her hand, she hugged it to her chest. Its head flopped forlornly over her arms. What was it about this man that made her feel so naked and exposed that she needed to keep something solid between them?

"Why not?" he asked. He was frowning at her, quietly implacable.

"Well . . . because . . ." She fumbled to a stop, then asked uncertainly, "You don't mean *private* lessons?"

"Yes, I do. At my house. My pool."

"Oh, no." She took a step backward, shaking her head firmly. "No, I really couldn't. It wouldn't be—"

Zack sighed. "Dorothy, haven't you noticed? This isn't Kansas. And I'm not the wicked witch of the West. I've got nothing in mind except teaching you to swim."

"Oh. Well, of course not. I mean . . ." How foolish of her to think . . . whatever she'd thought. She didn't know what to think, that was the problem. In fact, she felt very much as if she had been hit by a tornado. The idea of learning to swim was terrifying; the idea of Zack London's teaching her to swim was both terrifying and exhilarating. She licked dry lips and murmured, "I can't afford you."

His gaze was following the movement of her tongue across her lips, but his expression was carefully dispassionate. "Did I say anything about charges? I'd consider you a professional challenge."

She said faintly, "You're serious, aren't you?"

"Oh, yes." When she still felt as if she'd been turned to stone, he carefully removed Bosley from her clutches and took both of her cold hands in his. "Maddy . . . look. I told you before, I know it took courage for you to show up at that pool the other day. I admire you for that. I know what this must mean to you. You *need* to learn to swim, not just for all the usual reasons, but because you owe it to yourself.

And I'm the one who can teach you. If you'll trust me. Will you let me, Maddy? Please?"

She wanted to trust him. She did trust him, even though she wondered why it seemed so important to him that she learn to swim. Why should he care?

Then she wondered, why she should care what his motives were. She wanted so badly to learn to swim, to overcome her awful fear of water, and here one of the world's all-time great swimmers was offering— was begging—to teach her! And she really was sure she could trust him. She knew that a man still in the process of healing from a terrible emotional wound wasn't likely to be looking for new entanglements. So what was she hesitating for?

Besides, a thought had just struck her. Now that Theresa's case had been turned over to the proper authorities, there wouldn't be any reason for Zack to contact her again. That realization hit her with a sensation that felt a lot like panic.

"All right," she heard herself say. "I'll do it."

"Good girl. We can start . . . how's tomorrow evening? Early. Can you come right after work?"

She cleared her throat. "I have flexible hours."

"Six o'clock, then. Still plenty of daylight left." He grinned suddenly. "Although, come to think of it, there's no reason we couldn't do this at night. A pool can be beautiful at night, with the underwater lights on."

"Six is fine," Maddy said quickly, remembering the lighted pools she'd seen, and the crystal-clear view of the bodies in them. "Where do you live?"

"I'll draw you a map. It's up by the golf course; might be hard to find." He let go of her hands at last and picked up the pad and pencil by the telephone. After scribbling rapidly for a few minutes he tore the top sheet off the pad and handed it to her.

With a curious mixture of excitement and dread, Maddy took it and whispered, "Thank you."

"Now, don't flake out on me." He reached out to touch the side of her face. "Promise you'll come."

"I'll be there," she murmured absently. She'd just noticed that his eyelashes were very long. They didn't *look* long, because the tips were bleached golden. That seemed utterly fascinating to her. "I promise."

"You'd better be there. You're a personal challenge to me, you know, not just a professional one."

"What do you mean?" Perhaps she'd better pay attention. She was already beginning to wonder if she'd been wrong about his emotional condition.

"Yeah . . ." His thumb was lightly stroking her jaw, moving back and forth in an absent sort of way. He didn't even seem aware of what he was doing. "Someday, you know, you're going to trust me enough to tell me what happened to make you so afraid of water."

A shiver jolted Maddy, dispelling the last wisps of fog. "You seem awfully sure of yourself," she retorted.

"Oh, I am." His hand dropped away, and as he turned to go he added cryptically, "For the first time in a long, long time."

He left her shivering in a warm golden shaft of sunshine.

From his car, Zack looked thoughtfully back at the odd little house. With no windows, at least she couldn't look out and catch him gazing at her home like a smitten adolescent. And wouldn't *that* frighten her to death!

A stroke of genius, he thought, coming up with the swimming-lessons idea as a way to get past that guard of hers. Not only would she be vulnerable and dependent in the water, but it was one place she couldn't take along those damn puppets!

Though why he wanted to get closer to her he couldn't imagine. At first glance she'd seemed exactly the sort of woman he'd tried diligently to avoid these past few years. And yet . . . something about her made him think of lost puppies and orphaned kittens. Maybe because, as he'd told her, she really was a long, long way from Kansas. Or Indiana.

He had a feeling that, if he were ever really going to get close to her, he was going to have to help her find the way back.

Five

"She looks so little," Maddy said softly. "And so . . . alone." She turned from the one-way observation window. "Larry . . ."

"Maddy," Dr. Larry Whitlaw said warningly, and put a comforting arm across her shoulders. "Come on, now." He gave her a little squeeze.

She sighed. "Oh, Larry, I know. But . . ." Her voice trailed off as she watched Theresa work patiently with a puzzle in the Crisis Center's playroom.

"But you let yourself get involved here, didn't you?" Larry said. "After all my lectures, warnings, threats, and fatherly advice."

She smiled ruefully up at the Crisis Center's founder and director. "Yes, but not intentionally. Darn it, Larry, she had me hooked before I knew she was going to wind up here. What could I do?"

"Yeah, well." Larry Whitlaw stooped to look through the glass. He was a very tall, very thin man, whose poor posture did nothing to detract from his natural athletic grace. "She is a cutie, isn't she?"

Maddy cleared her throat. "I'm a little surprised you

had her brought in so quickly. Was the family environment that bad?"

Larry frowned. "It wasn't good. Theresa doesn't live with her parents. They're both dead, as a matter of fact. She lives with an aunt and uncle. The mother's sister, I believe. The aunt is okay—just scared to death of her husband, which is fairly typical."

"Umm." Maddy nodded and tried to sound no more than professionally interested. She knew she wasn't fooling Larry one bit. "So what's going to be done with her? Will she become a county ward?"

"Larry nodded. "Hope so—hearing's tomorrow."

"Who's the judge?" When she thought of Theresa facing so many strangers in cold and unfamiliar places, something stirred inside her, awakening fierce and primitive instincts. She felt an urge to shelter, and to protect.

"Donna Bergman." Larry's compassion-weary eyes twinkled down at Maddy with understanding. "I put in a special request."

Maddy was relieved on that point, at least. Judge Bergman was a warm, motherly-looking person with a knack for putting traumatized children, as well as the adult victims of rape and abuse, at ease. "What about the aunt and uncle? Will they contest?"

"I doubt it. The aunt seems to have been genuinely fond of her sister, and tried to do what she could for the kid, but between you and me, I think she'll be relieved to have the source of tension between her and her husband out of the house. No, I don't anticipate any problems."

"So . . . what then?" Maddy persisted. "Where is she staying in the meantime? Juvenile Hall?" She was finding it increasingly hard to push her voice past the knot in her throat. Inside the playroom, Theresa had finished her puzzle. As she was carrying it back to the shelf, she stumbled, jostling the tray and spilling wooden puzzle pieces across the linoleum floor. Maddy could hear the clatter even through the thick walls and double-glass window. Tears stung her nose and throat as she watched the little girl clap both hands over her mouth and look around with huge, terrified eyes, then kneel and begin to gather the pieces with quick, furtive movements. The back of her neck looked so fragile, so vulnerable.

"Juvenile Hall's impacted at the moment," Larry said. "She'll stay at the Crisis Shelter until we can find her a foster home." His voice sounded thoughtful, and Maddy glanced up, not surprised to find he was looking straight at her, not at Theresa.

To her own amazement she heard herself say, "Larry, let me keep her."

"Maddy . . ." He looked sympathetic but regretful—and not nearly as startled by the request as Maddy was.

"It's so *cold* here," she said. "So . . . institutional. She's got to be feeling lost and confused. Just until you find a good foster home."

"Maddy, you know what my thoughts are on this. You know what the policy—"

"Oh, Larry, damn the policy! That's a little *child* in there. She knows me. She trusts me. I know she'd be happier—"

"For how long? Two days? A week? She forms an attachment to you, and then she's got to adjust to another change. And *you*—do you really think it would be easier for you to let her go *then*?"

Maddy took a deep breath. "Then let me be her foster home. Come on, Larry, why not?"

The psychologist made an exasperated sound and turned away from the window. "Maddy . . ."

She gripped the sleeve of his rumpled tweed jacket. "Larry, if you put in a recommendation—"

"I don't see how I could do that, Maddy."

"*Why?*"

"Maddy, you're not seeing things very clearly. Which is precisely why you shouldn't have allowed yourself to get involved emotionally in a case. To begin with, you're single, a working woman, with no experience with children."

"No experience! What about my work here at the clinic? What about my programs in the schools? I see hundreds of children!"

"*See* them, sure. But that's not living with them. Raising them. Dealing with the everyday problems—the tears and tantrums, the mess, the noise, the inconvenience. And most of all, the constant and unremitting responsibility."

"Don't lecture me, Larry. I'm not a child, and I think I know very well what that little girl needs. She needs a lot of love and patience and affection, and I think I can give it to her!"

"Maddy." Larry's eyes and voice were kind. "What Theresa needs more than anything is a normal home environment. Can you honestly tell me you could provide her with that? The way you live? In a fairy-tale cottage, surrounded by talking toys and a cat with a weird sense of humor? You know the standards for foster homes as well as I do. Honey, you can't give her a bedroom to sleep in. *You* don't even have a bedroom to sleep in!"

Maddy just stared at him, frustrated by her yearnings and the knowledge that he was right. After a moment Larry pursed his lips and asked softly, "And then what happens . . . when she's adopted?"

"Adopted?"

"If no other relatives can be located, we'll push to have Theresa released for permanent adoption. As a matter of fact, we've already had an inquiry about Theresa, from someone interested in permanent custody."

"Someone's asked about adopting Theresa? Already?" Maddy was stunned. "Who? Who could possibly know she'd be—"

"Someone you might have heard of, actually." Larry's face was carefully blank. "Zack London."

"*What?*" Maddy's voice rose to an incredulous

squeak. "You can't be serious!" Of all the emotions bumping into one another inside her, the most recognizable were jealousy and a sense of betrayal. He knew how she felt about Theresa. Why hadn't he said anything to her about this yesterday?

Larry was gazing placidly at her. "Sure am. Came to see me this morning, as a matter of fact. Of course, I told him he was a bit premature—"

"Premature! Larry, he's no more qualified to be a parent than I am! You don't mean to tell me he'd be seriously considered—"

Larry looked stern. "On the contrary, Maddy, he's a lot more qualified than you are. He's at least had experience raising a child. He's financially secure, and capable of providing materially for a child."

"He's single!"

"That's true," Larry murmured, nodding sagely. "That's true. But not likely to remain so forever. Once he's had some time to heal—"

"How do you know? About Zack London, I mean? You sound as if you know him personally."

"Oh, Zack and I have worked together on various projects—Boy's Club, Parks and Rec." Larry shrugged and smiled.

Feeling frustrated and outwitted, Maddy abruptly turned her back on Larry and began stuffing puppets into their cases with uncharacteristic disregard for their well-being.

"Hey . . . Maddy, listen." Larry Whitlaw was a good friend, and when he placed his big hands gently on her shoulders her anger at him ebbed. Her shoulders sagged, and he massaged them sympathetically. "You know that if anybody else did this, I'd put 'em on leave of absence, don't you? Emotional basket cases we don't need around here."

She shook his hands off and laughed painfully. "So what makes me an exception?"

He waved a hand at the puppet cases. "At the risk of making you impossible to live with, I guess a lot of people around here think you're damn near irreplaceable."

She placed a hand over her heart and groaned. "*Please.* I don't think my ego can stand it!"

He chuckled, and gazed fondly at her for a moment. "Tell you what. I don't see any harm in your maintaining contact with Theresa, once she's established in her foster home. I've no objection to a friendly relationship, as long as it doesn't interfere with her adjustment to her new environment and isn't disruptive to her or the foster parents. Is that understood?"

"Understood," Maddy said softly, and smiled radiantly.

But as she loaded her puppets into her car, she was thinking, with an acknowledged lack of fairness, *Zack London, how could you do this to me?*

It was probably a good thing Maddy was still angry with Zack when she arrived at his home for her first swimming lesson. Without that spine-stiffening core of resentment, she might never have made it from her car to the front door. As it was, the finger that punched the doorbell shook noticeably. Maddy noticed it, and clenched her hand into a fist. Lord, how she wished she'd brought one of her puppets along! Bosley would have known exactly how to deal with this. . . .

A moment later she was thinking that Bosley, in her new incarnation, at least, would have had a field day.

Zack opened the door himself. He was wearing only a pair of swimming trunks and a light blue cotton something with a hood. The blue thing—a light jacket or cover-up of some sort—was unzipped and hanging negligently off his broad shoulders. His chest, torso, and those long, smooth-muscled swimmer's legs were bare. Maddy stared resentfully at him. Why couldn't he have had a maid? His house, like all the houses in this part of town, was big, custom-built, and overlooked the golf course. She would have thought Zack London at least would have a *maid*.

He, in his turn, was looking her up and down, taking in her neat navy blue linen slacks and white cable-knit cotton sweater. "Hi. Glad you came," he said with amusement in his voice and eyes. "Did you come to swim, or ski?"

"It gets *cold* in the evenings," she said defensively, clutching her oversized purse tightly. "And I don't make a habit of driving around town in a bathing suit."

He mumbled something that sounded like "Pity," and stood aside. "Come on in. You can change in the bathroom."

"Thank you," she said primly. Her teeth had developed a tendency to chatter. She clamped them together firmly and said brightly, "Nice place." She waved a hand that encompassed both Zack's manicured front lawn and the golf course beyond it. "Do you play golf?"

"Not much." His expression and voice were neutral. "Carol—my wife—played quite a bit."

"Oh." In her dismay, Maddy forgot to keep her teeth clenched. Sure enough, they made an audible clattering noise.

Zack glanced at her with interest. "Are you really that cold, or is it nerves?"

"Cold," she mumbled, hugging herself and lying with conviction. "Definitely."

"Uh-huh." Zack's expression was carefully serious. "Well, it would probably help if you came in off my front doorstep."

"Doorstep?" she looked around, surprised to find that she was still outside. "Oh . . ."

Zack held the door, politely waiting. Maddy stayed where she was. After a moment Zack sighed, took her arm, and pulled her across the threshold.

"Nice house," she said, looking around desperately.

The living room was enormous, immaculate, and sterile, done in neutrals and cool shades of blue and sea green. Beyond it she could see a formal dining room, raised two steps above the level of the entryway and living room. It, too, was immaculate. It seemed unused, like a display in a furniture-store window. "It seems very . . . big."

"Too big for one person, you're probably thinking. And you're right." Zack's jaw seemed to tighten, then relax. "I'm thinking seriously about doing something about that."

Maddy's breath caught in her throat. "Do you . . . live here . . . all alone?" It was hard to imagine someone as casual-appearing as Zack, with his jeans and polo shirts, his undisciplined hair and sunburned skin, living in a place as cold and empty as this. Maddy hated to think of Theresa living in such an environment. And surely the county-adoption caseworker would agree that this was no place for a child.

"I have a housekeeper." Zack's voice was dry. Maddy glanced at him guiltily and saw a sardonic smile on his lips. "So you don't have to worry about being alone with me. And now," he said briskly, dismissing that subject and putting his hands on her shoulders, turning her the way one would a confused and balky child, "quit stalling. Bathroom's down that hall—first door on your right. Did you bring a towel?"

She snapped her fingers. "Oops—I left it in the car. I'll just go—"

Zack's arm made a barrier across the door just in time to thwart her escape. "No, you don't. I think I can probably find you something." His eyes were amused, but sympathetic.

"I'm sorry," she muttered, feeling ridiculous. "I guess maybe I am a little nervous."

"*No!*" He put a hand on his chest and looked incredulous.

She stared resentfully at him for a long, tense

moment, then gave an embarrassed giggle. "Okay, I'm sorry," she said. "Really. I'm being pretty silly."

"Yeah, you are." He put his hands on her shoulders and smiled disarmingly at her. "Do I look like a maniac who drowns gorgeous blonds in my hot tub?"

She focused on his dimple and shook her head. "No."

"Oh, what a relief." His smile broadened and became irresistible. "Besides, Dahlia wouldn't allow it. Maddy . . . look. I'm here to help you get over your fears, not make them worse. Everything we do tonight will be pleasant. Enjoyable. Even . . . fun." His voice was soft and deep-throated. It soothed the rough, raw edges of her fear like warm oil. "Trust me. Nothing's going to hurt you tonight, or scare you. Okay?"

"Okay." She nodded, but somewhat dubiously. She did trust him not to hurt her. So why was she still shivering?

It wasn't until she was closed into the privacy of the bathroom and facing her own reflection in the mirror that she realized it wasn't the water she was afraid of at all. It was Zack. Just . . . Zack.

The problem, she decided as she peeled off her sweater and folded it neatly, was that he kept giving off conflicting signals. Not that she was adept at reading such signals, granted, but she'd had enough of the wrong kind of experience to know when a man was putting the make on her. She just wasn't hearing the usual warning bells and sirens with Zack. And yet he'd already taken more physical liberties with her than she'd tolerated from any of the men she'd dated in recent memory.

What did he want from her? On the one hand, he courted her trust. And on the other . . . *what?*

Maddy pulled on her suit, the plain black one she had bought for her first lesson at the public pool, and surveyed herself critically in the mirror. Damn the suit, anyway. It had seemed so practical. She'd had no idea when she bought it that it would be so . . . revealing.

"You really are cold, aren't you?" Zack said when she finally found the courage to rejoin him. She glanced down at herself and groaned inwardly.

"Don't worry," he went on. "The hot tub will take care of those chills." He sounded comforting. Maddy tried to hide her telltale nipples behind a folded towel.

"H-hot tub?" She stumbled a little as she followed Zack down a short flight of carpeted stairs to a sumptuously appointed room that appeared to be a combination den and game room. The carpet was thick, chairs and sofas big and comfortable, tables cluttered with books and magazines. One end of the room was dominated by a huge stone fireplace, the other by an equally enormous pool table. In between, wide glass doors opened onto a covered patio made jungly by potted and hanging plants. Beyond the greenery, Maddy could just see the turquoise glitter of the pool.

"We'll *start* with the hot tub," Zack said, pulling open the sliding glass doors. His hand on her back was uncompromising. With a perfectly straight face he added, "It's a terrific way to warm up."

"Hot tub," she repeated, balking suspiciously. "I thought you were supposed to teach me to swim." She glared at him accusingly. "I may be from Indiana, but I know you can't swim in a hot tub."

"Hey, who's the teacher here? Quit worrying about the swimming part. Right now it's your fear of water we have to deal with. First things first. And the first thing I'm going to do"—he firmly removed the towel from her frozen fingers and dropped it onto the deck's rough paving stones—"is show you some of the *sensual* properties of water." His jacket joined her towel.

"Sen-sensual?" Inexplicably, Maddy had begun to shiver again.

Zack moved away to flip switches and punch buttons. He returned to hold out his hand to her in a gesture that was very much like an invitation to dance.

"Yes . . . sensual. As in, 'appealing to the senses.' Your fear of water isn't all-encompassing. You don't get hysterical when presented with a glass of iced tea, do you?"

"Of course not!"

"And you take showers, don't you?"

"Yes, of course I do. That's ridic—"

"We're making progress! Baths?"

"Yes!"

"You see? We've just got to narrow the scope of your fear even further. If we eliminate all the things about water that *don't* frighten you, let's hope that, by the process of elimination, we can get to what's really bugging you. Come on, Maddy—take my hand."

Fascinated against her will, she put her hand in his larger, warmer one, and allowed herself to be led to the edge of the tub.

He stopped and murmured, "Listen."

"What?" She stared at him, confused.

"Hush. Listen to the water. Hearing's a sense, too. Don't you know that the sound of running water is considered to be a terrific natural tranquilizer?" Keeping a firm grip on her hand, he stepped into the bubbling water. Maddy had no choice but to follow.

"Ever been in a hot tub before?" he asked casually as he guided her into the whirlpool bath.

She threw him what she hoped was a disdainful look. "Of course I have. I didn't just fall off a hay wagon, you know!"

He grinned disarmingly and peered closely at her. "Let's see." He picked an imaginary straw out of her hair, shook his head, and flicked it away. Maddy found herself grinning back, and curled her free hand into a fist and pounded it once, in gentle reproof, on his smooth chest. He captured it and, holding both of her hands between his, said softly, "Maddy, sit down."

Without taking her eyes from his, she lowered herself into the frothy bubbles. Warmth, churning, caressing, tingling warmth enveloped her to her chin.

Maddy hadn't lied. She had been in hot tubs before. But not like this. She wasn't sure why, but this was . . . different. The sensations were indescribable. And delicious. The water stroked her body like fingers, magical, sensitive fingers. And the churning seemed to be inside her. . . .

Zack's mouth had curved in a smile, but as she gazed at him it seemed to blur and soften. He let go of her hands and touched her face, drawing his thumb across the film of moisture on her upper lip. Her lips parted in response. He touched her warm cheek with the backs of his fingers, then lifted a strand of her hair and delicately tucked it behind her ear.

"Maddy . . . close your eyes."

It was an easy command to obey. Her eyelids had grown so heavy, it was almost a relief to let them drift softly down.

"Feel the water . . . go with it. Let it hold you. . . ."

His fingers combed her hair back from her temples, fanning wide to encompass her head. Her head had become too heavy for her neck to support. It felt good to let it lie in the basket of his hands.

"Don't go to sleep on me, now." His voice was gently amused.

Her eyes flew open, and for a moment she felt disoriented to discover it was still daylight. Her senses had somehow evoked subliminal memories of tropical nights, soft and humid and heavy with the scent of flowers. She cleared her throat, and, like an intoxicated person trying hard to appear sober, focused her eyes on Zack's dimple and said, "I wasn't sleeping."

Her intention was to speak clearly and with authority, but for some reason her words came out with a bit of a slur. She knotted her eyebrows into a frown and tried again. "I was just . . . relaxing."

"Good." His smile was approving. His fingers moved, rubbing back and forth on her scalp. The rasping sound they made was loud in her ears, and had an oddly hypnotic effect. Her jaw felt unhinged. She said "Umm . . ." then decided that it took too much effort to talk.

"Now," Zack murmured, "I want you to lie in the water. Raise your body, stretch out flat, just like you would if you were lying in bed. The most comfortable bed in the world. Feathers . . . down . . ."

"Water bed," she mumbled, pleased with her cleverness.

Zack's chuckle made a cool stirring on her heated skin. Still supporting her head in his hands, he turned her and arranged himself so that her back was against his chest, her head resting in the hollow of his shoulder. His hands slid down her neck to her shoulders, then moved slowly along her arms to her wrists. Very gently he drew her arms up and out until they lay on the water's frothy surface, perpendicular to her body.

"That's right . . . just let them float. Let the water hold you."

She felt his hands on her back, her ribs, her waist, gently lifting. They seemed like part of the water. . . .

It was weird, as if she were floating on clouds of fragrant steam, but at the same time her body felt so *heavy*. She was aware of her pulse throbbing in strange and disturbing places, in parts of her body she'd never noticed her pulse in before. She had a vague feeling that what she was doing, what *he* was doing, was more erotic than educational, but she couldn't seem to care. In fact, if she turned her head just a little, her lips would touch wet-silk warmth . . . his neck. . . .

"Oops," Zack said. "It's getting too hot in here, I think." Odd, she thought. Was it her ears, or did his voice seem slurred too? "Time to cool off. Upsy-daisy."

He restored her to a sitting position. She felt light-headed and slightly nauseated.

"Can you stand?" he asked.

She nodded, and did so, but her legs felt like jelly and she had to lean heavily on the hand he offered to help her over the side of the tub and into the pool.

"It'll seem cold," he said, "after the hot tub."

It did, but it also felt refreshing, like a cool drink on a hot summer's day. The water was a liquid caress on her heated skin. It touched and tantalized her nerve endings in new ways, and gave another dimension to the term "gooseflesh." Maddy forgot she was in a swimming pool. All she was aware of was the cool kiss of the water and Zack.

He was there, close behind her, his hands curving around her shoulders, his chest against her back. His words were a whisper in her ear.

"Now, do what you did in the tub. Stretch out . . . just like lying in bed. Relax. Let the water hold you."

This time he didn't have to position her arms. She let them drift outward on the gently undulating water, like wings. And her head came to rest quite naturally in the curve of his neck. Once again his hands were on her waist, lifting, but now the water was cold and his hands were warm, and there was no confusing the two. She felt his body come up against her back and align itself under hers, and she knew beyond any doubt that it was his body that supported her, not the water. She felt her hair fan out around her shoulders and tickle her skin with a feather's touch. Zack's chin was a solid, raspy pressure against her temple, her anchor and her security. She could have drifted like that forever.

Her legs settled slowly downward, until they tangled with Zack's hard, masculine ones. She jerked hers upward, but that caused her middle to sink. When her bottom encountered an approximately corresponding section of his anatomy, she panicked, and floundered to an upright position. Zack's arms came around her and held her tightly against him.

"Take it easy," he said tersely against her ear. "It's okay."

"I'm all right," she said irritably. "I'm *fine*." She didn't tell him that it wasn't the water that had precipitated her panic. She tilted her head forward so that his lips were touching her hair, and not the supersensitive shell of her ear. She felt his mouth move briefly down along the lines of her neck. Then he put his hands on her shoulders and stood back, separating himself from her.

"Good job. You did great." His voice sounded strange, oddly garbled. "And that's enough for one day, I think."

Maddy thought so too. She felt shaky, and again knew it had very little to do with her fear of water. In fact, she'd hardly thought about her fear at all.

Quite suddenly, she didn't want to look at Zack. She was vibrantly, electrifyingly aware of him with every nerve and sense she possessed, and was afraid he would see it in her face if she looked at him. Dammit, it was his fault. In fact, he'd done it deliberately, showing her the "sensual properties of water"! The trouble was, how did she turn her senses off now that she was out of the water?

He gave her his hand to guide her up the pool steps. His hand was firm and strong, and she was sorry when he released her and bent to pick up two beach towels from the deck. As he tossed her one, she noticed that he didn't seem eager to meet her eyes, either. He was wearing that same perplexed frown she'd seen on his face the day she'd appeared by mistake in his swim class. She was just beginning to feel as shy and awkward as she had then, when he suddenly looked full at her and smiled. To Maddy, it was as if someone had turned on a high-powered heat lamp.

"Well, that wasn't so terrible, was it?" he asked. All at once he seemed to be bursting with energy and good spirits.

She shook her head. He was making her breathless

again. "No. But I didn't—we didn't *do* anything. I thought . . ."

"Thought what? That I was going to just toss you in the deep end of the pool and let you sink or swim?"

It was a joking remark, but it caught Maddy off guard. She couldn't control her involuntary spasm of reaction. She saw Zack's eyes narrow slightly and knew he hadn't missed it, but he didn't comment. Instead he stepped close to her, took her towel, and arranged it around her shoulders, using one end of it to dab at the moisture on his own face. It was an unexpected gesture, and one of such complete familiarity that it seemed to link them together in a cozy intimacy that excluded everything but the two of them. Everything—even breathing—was suspended. His eyes were very intense, and so near, she couldn't focus on both of them at once. She could see the tiny amber specks in the deep blue irises, count the drops of moisture on his eyelashes. His body was heat, strength, and magnetism, pulling on her.

She heard a small, sharply indrawn breath, and realized it was hers. It broke some sort of spell. Smile lines crinkled around Zack's eyes.

"I'm your teacher, remember? You done good—trust me." He ducked his head and dropped a quick, and completely fraternal, kiss on the end of her nose. "Come on. Let's dry off, and I'll see if Dahlia's around. Would you like some coffee? Hot cocoa? Herb tea?"

"*Herb tea?*"

He shrugged, grinning. "Hey, we aim to please."

Laughing, Maddy said, "Coffee's fine." And then, impulsively, "No—hot cocoa. I don't think I've had hot cocoa since I was a little girl." She drew the towel around herself, snuggling into its folds and into her memories. "It makes me think of snow and cold winter evenings. We'd come in half-frozen, and Mother would have a big pot of cocoa steaming on the stove. One sip, and you could feel the warmth clear down to your toes."

Zack dropped his arm casually across her shoulders and said softly, "Hot cocoa it is." As they went into the house he raised his voice to call up the stairs, "Dahlia? Dahlia, are you there?"

A rich and mellow voice answered, with just a touch of gentle mockery, "Yes, Zachary."

"Dahlia, come here a minute. Want you to meet a friend of mine. I'm in the basement."

"I can *hear* where you are," the voice scolded good-naturedly, coming nearer. A very tall, very regal woman with white hair and toffee-colored skin appeared at the top of the stairs, drying her hands on a towel.

"Dahlia, this is Maddy." Maddy was very aware of Zack's hands resting on her shoulders in a gesture that seemed almost . . . possessive.

The housekeeper's dark gaze met Zack's eyes first, then took in the position of his hands, and finally swept over Maddy with a look of frank assessment. "Hello, Maddy." Her voice had a low, musical quality, like an oboe.

"I'm teaching Maddy to swim," Zack said, explaining, it seemed to Maddy, unnecessarily.

Dahlia said "Hmm," and looked dubious. Her expression plainly said, "A likely story . . ."

Maddy turned her head to look at Zack and found the expression on his face so patently guilty that it began to strike her as funny. It was strangely comforting to see Zachary London—*Aquaman!*—looking like a little boy caught with frogs in his pocket and mischief on his mind. Her self-confidence seemed to be growing in direct proportion to his discomfort. It made a warm, cozy pool inside her, very much like that hot cocoa she remembered so well. And at the same time, it gave her an overwhelming desire to giggle.

Zack cleared his throat. "Dahl, could you please make us some . . . hot cocoa?"

"*Hot cocoa?*" The housekeeper's eyebrows shot up.

"Hot cocoa," Zack confirmed solemnly.

"Hot cocoa," Dahlia said, and went away muttering to herself.

When she was out of earshot, Maddy released her pent-up laughter and murmured, "Wow."

Zack look puzzled. "What's funny?" She shook her head and covered her smile with her hand. Her feelings were too tender and new to bring into full light.

"Dahlia raised eight children," he said, still watching her warily. "Every single one of them went to college."

"Hmm," Maddy said, and sat, gingerly because of her wet bathing suit, on one of the two couches that flanked the fireplace. She didn't feel tender anymore, and she didn't feel like laughing, either. It had occurred to her that Zack's housekeeper was better equipped and qualified to care for a child than she was. To ward off creeping depression, she looked around her and said brightly, "This is a nice room. It's . . . warm. Lived in."

"Whereas the rest of the house isn't," Zack said dryly, sweeping newspapers onto the floor as he sat opposite her. "There's a good reason for that, actually." He leaned back and propped his feet on the oak parquet coffee table. "This is where I live." His gaze rested briefly on Maddy's hands, which she was using to hold the towel firmly together over her breasts. "Except for my bedroom, it's the only room in the house I really use." His smile was crooked. "As you pointed out, it's a big place for one person, and it makes things easier on Dahlia. Maddy . . ." He took his feet off the coffee table and sat forward, looking earnest. "There's something . . ."

Maddy felt cold settle over her. She didn't know why she dreaded what was coming, but she did. Somehow, just knowing what he was going to say filled her with a deep sense of loss.

He got up and walked to the fireplace. With his back

to her he took a deep breath. Maddy set her jaw and waited. Finally, he turned to face her.

"Maddy, what would you think . . . about my adopting Theresa?"

Six

Adopt Theresa.

Even with advance warning, hearing Zack say the words out loud made Maddy feel queasy. Hurt. Resentful. *Jealous.*

And she couldn't figure out why, or why she should have this sense of loss. It had been foolish to think that *she* might have had any chance to adopt Theresa. It was a dumb idea anyway. Larry had been absolutely right about that. And the funny thing was, Maddy didn't even know where it had sprung from. She was only twenty-five, for Pete's sake! She wasn't even thinking of getting married, wasn't dating anyone in particular. She *liked* living alone. Well . . . almost alone. Why this sudden yearning for motherhood?

Zack was talking to her, though it seemed more as if he were talking to himself. "Maybe it's crazy. I *know* it's crazy." He raked his fingers through his hair and shook his head, looking perplexed. "I mean, I've only seen her a couple of times. And it's not like I've been thinking about it. In fact, it's probably been about the furthest thing from my mind. But . . . I don't know, there was just something about that little girl, right from the first time I saw her, that day at the pool, remember?"

Maddy nodded dumbly. As if she would ever forget it!

Zack gave a short, ironic laugh. "When you told me to keep an eye on her, and why, I felt . . . strange. Kind of sick to my stomach, you know what I mean? And then, when I saw her . . ." His fingers tore through his hair, leaving wreckage behind. His eyes were dark and passionate, his jaw bunched with tension. With his broken nose he looked like a street brawler, spoiling for a fight. Maddy was fascinated. He resembled that all-American sunshine boy of billboards and cereal boxes about as much as she resembled Cher.

"I wanted to kill someone," he said through clenched teeth. "Really *kill* someone—with my bare hands." He looked at Maddy. "Can you understand that? And it was like . . . I just *knew*. You know?" His eyes were focusing on her with such naked appeal that she had to look away to save her own emotions. Without the protection of her puppets, she felt . . . bruised.

You know? she repeated silently. Oh, boy, did she know! As she stared through a shimmering blur at the mess on the coffee table, she was thinking that, when it came to falling in love, whether it was with a member of the opposite sex, a lonely little girl, or a puppy in a pet shop window, you really didn't have much to say about it. Your heart did as it pleased. The rest of you just went along for the ride. And sometimes it was a very bumpy ride.

"Maddy?" Zack was sitting down on the couch opposite her, looking puzzled. She realized she hadn't yet answered his question, or, in fact, said a word. She cleared her throat and offered a tentative "Umm."

"Look, I know you probably think it's crazy. A bachelor adopting a little girl. And I understand that—you don't really know me very well." He jumped up, too full of tension and energy to sit still. "But it's different now. Single people can adopt kids. Happens all the time, right?"

"Well . . ."

"Anyway, I thought you might know—" He came back to the couch and perched on the edge of it. "Maddy, you work with those agencies all the time. Tell me honestly, do you think I can do it? Is there any chance at all that they will let me adopt her?"

"Well, I—"

Maddy was given a reprieve by Dahlia, who arrived at that moment bearing two mugs of steaming cocoa on a tray. As she set the mugs on the coffee table she divided a look of stern disapproval equally between Maddy and Zack and went back up the stairs grumbling about people who sat around in wet clothes, catching their deaths.

Maddy picked up a mug and curled her hands around it, inhaling the heavenly scent of chocolate. She was feeling a little ashamed now, and a lot confused. Somehow, during the course of the evening, this man sitting across the coffee table from her had stopped being Aquaman, once and for all. He'd even stopped being Zack London, Olympic champion and household name. He'd become just a man—a very strong, very attractive, very *vulnerable* man. And she was finding out that that made him an even more devastating threat to her emotional stability. She was less in awe of him, but somehow even more afraid. She wanted less and less to keep him at a safe distance, an arm's—or puppet's—length away. She wanted instead to reach out and touch him. To touch his face, to brush back that stubborn curl of sunburnished hair from his forehead. That confused her, because she'd never felt like that about anyone before.

And she felt ashamed because she knew how selfish she was being. Theresa had lost her parents; Zack had lost his child. Theresa needed love; Zack had plenty of it to give. It should have seemed like the happiest ending to a sad story since Cinderella. It was childish of her to feel left out.

"You haven't said much," he observed, absently sipping his cocoa. "You're frowning. I guess you don't think much of the idea."

"Oh," she mumbled, taking a deep breath, "it isn't that."

"What, then?" He shook his head. "I guess I thought you'd be happier about it."

Anger flared in her. How could he be so insensitive! Didn't he have any idea how she felt? She tried to remember if she ever had mentioned to Zack the way she felt about Theresa. Well, no, probably not. She hadn't told him anything about herself, really. She didn't know him well enough.

Taking another deep breath, she said, "I'm just surprised. It's very . . . sudden. And unexpected."

"I know. It is for me too." He was watching her closely. Maddy braced herself and met his eyes, then leaned into the contact, pressing against it, testing the strength of her emotions.

She swallowed. "And, um . . . you're single."

His gaze didn't waver. "Yes, I am. But I don't intend to be single forever. And in the meantime, I have Dahlia."

"Yes, that's another thing. What does she think of all this? Have you talked to her?"

"Yes, I have, and she's tickled to death." Maddy tried to imagine that majestic woman being "tickled" about anything. "She's ready to take on the entire county, *and* that jerk of an uncle, single-handed!" *That*, Maddy thought, sounded more like the Dahlia she'd met.

She leaned forward and said earnestly, "Zack, it isn't that I think it's a bad idea. I just don't think it's a good idea to get your hopes up. Theresa is only in temporary protective custody—a seventy-two-hour warrant. Tomorrow she'll be made a temporary ward of the court. There will be witnesses. The guardians have to appear."

"I know," Zack said, looking grim. "I've been subpoenaed as a witness."

Maddy nodded. "So have I. I guess I'll see you there. . . ." Her voice, somehow, just trailed off. Maintaining eye contact with Zack became uncomfortable, so she broke it and stood up, pulling her towel tightly around her. "She'll be put in a foster home; there will be a thorough search for other relatives. And after that, *if* nobody turns up, the current guardians would have to sign papers relinquishing all claim. And you'd probably have to get them to agree to a private adoption in advance of the permanent-custody hearing. That way, there would be a transfer of custody directly to you, rather than to the county. Once she's made a permanent county ward, it's very difficult to—"

"*Damn* difficult!" Zack jumped up and followed her to the cold fireplace. When she turned to face him, he put his hands on her arms. "Just tell me what I have to do."

Maddy suddenly felt small and unprotected. She was surprised to discover it wasn't altogether a bad feeling. "Well," she said, smiling slightly, "for starters, I'd get a lawyer."

"I have one." Zack brushed that impatiently aside. "What else?"

"You've already got Larry Whitlaw on your side. That helps."

Zack looked at her speculatively. "You've already talked with Larry about this."

She nodded.

He was silent for a moment, then asked, "What about you? Are you on my side?" His voice was soft.

He touched the side of her face, then fingered a strand of damp hair back behind her ear.

Light shivers ran through her scalp and down her neck, just under her skin. She felt an urge to tilt her head and nuzzle her cheek against his hand. "Yes," she whispered. It was a kind of sigh. "Of course I'm on your side."

His triumphant laughter woke her from the sensual daze his nearness had induced. She muttered something vague about its being time to go and ran up the stairs to the bathroom where she had left her clothes.

Oh, yes, she was on his side. She'd do anything for that man. She'd just realized that, and it scared her a bit. She'd do what she could to help him win custody of Theresa, even though she wanted the little girl so badly herself, she ached with it.

Oh, be honest with yourself, Amanda, she thought as she drove home through the winding streets that bordered the golf course. You know what you really want!

She tried it on in her imagination, and it made a lovely vision through her tears, haloed in a pink shimmer of sunset: a dark-haired little girl smiling happily up at the two people on either side of her; one hand lost in the brawny grip of a man with powerful, swimmer's legs and unruly hair frosted with gold; the other held securely in the hand of a tall woman with Nordic coloring and a touch of self-consciousness in her walk. . . .

Zack wasn't looking forward to the hearing. He didn't know what to expect, but had a vague idea he ought to be making a good impression, so he'd put on a sport jacket and a tie.

He'd even gotten a haircut, in a last-ditch effort to subdue his hair. As far as he could see, it hadn't done anything but leave a telltale strip of untanned skin on the back of his neck, letting the whole world know just exactly what he'd tried to do.

"Relax," Larry Whitlaw told him as they were crossing the courtyard of the county building complex. "It's routine. The judge will ask a few questions, you answer in simple sentences, and that's it."

"Yeah, sure." Zack hadn't been in a courtroom since the day he'd faced a judge in juvenile traffic court about his first—and last—speeding ticket. He didn't remember it as having been a particularly pleasant experience. The judge had bawled him out and given him a choice of paying a fine or going to traffic school and having his driving record wiped clean. It hadn't been a hard decision to make. And then his dad had taken the fine out of his allowance anyway, and impounded his car keys for two weeks to boot.

That had been another time, another place, another courthouse, but Zack had an idea they were all pretty much alike. Big, dim, cold, and intimidating—a hell of a place for a little, tiny kid. He said as much to Larry.

The psychologist threw him a look as he dodged a gardener with a leaf blower. "Oh, Theresa won't be in the courtroom. The judge will talk to her privately in chambers." He raised his voice above the noise of the blower. "You won't even see Theresa today."

"Oh." Zack was surprised at how disappointed he was. "I don't see how a judge's chambers are much better," he said irritably. "It still seems like a hell of a thing for a little kid to have to face all alone."

"Don't worry about her," Larry said, chuckling. "I know what you're thinking, but believe me, Theresa will be okay. Judge Bergman's chambers happen to be about as depressing and intimidating as a bowlful of daffodils. And besides, she'll have Maddy with her, and probably another caseworker—"

"Maddy?" Zack halted in the middle of the courtyard beside a huge fountain inlaid with Spanish tile.

Larry checked his long stride and looked back at him, frowning at the interruption.

"Yeah, Maddy Gordon. Know her?"

"As a matter of fact, yes. We met at the pool. She's the one who told me to keep an eye on—"

"That's right. I'd forgotten." Larry snapped his fingers and took off again at his top speed—a loose-jointed lope. "Great girl . . . terrific with the kids. Uses puppets." He beamed at Zack over his shoulder.

Zack had to stretch some to catch up. "Yeah, I know."

Larry held the courthouse door open wide. He was trying hard to keep his expression innocent. "Let's see. . . . How long's it been since Carol died?"

Zack threw him a look. "Two years. Why?"

All Larry would say was "Hmm," as he sprinted for the elevator. Zack caught up with him in time to squeeze through the closing doors. In silence they watched the numbers above the door light up, one by one.

"I'm giving her swimming lessons," Zack announced as the bell dinged for the fourth floor.

"Good for you," Larry murmured placidly, bolting through the door and down the hall.

Zack felt a lot better, knowing Maddy was going to be with Theresa. Larry was right—she was good with kids. He remembered the way Theresa had clung to her instinctively that day at the pool. In fact, he remembered everything about the way they'd looked together, with Theresa's great big owl-eyes peering at him, and her head just about on a level with Maddy's thighs. . . .

Well, he was glad she was here—for Theresa's sake.

He actually managed to sustain that fiction until the moment she walked into the courtroom.

She was wearing tan slacks and a short-sleeved pink sweater, something so soft and fuzzy-looking, it made him want to cuddle it. Her hair . . . She really didn't wear it in any particular style, nothing faddish or trendy, anyway. It just hung there, down to where it brushed her shoulders, and when she moved, it swung with a silky ripple that reminded him of ripe wheat blowing in the wind. Everything about her made him want to *touch.*

"Hi, Larry," she said. She sat down next to the psychologist, then leaned across him to add in a breathy whisper, "Hi, Zack." Her cheeks were flushed and her mouth looked soft. Zack found, to his dismay, that he wanted to touch that part of her too.

She smiled at him, mercifully unaware of the images in his head, and murmured, "You've worn a tie." She seemed to want to say something else, but at that moment there was a small commotion at the back of the courtroom. Maddy glanced over her shoulder, then quickly faced front.

"That's the uncle and aunt," she said in a low voice. "Doesn't look as though they've brought counsel."

"Told you they wouldn't contest," Larry said smugly. "We'll be out of here in ten minutes."

Zack had told himself he wouldn't look at the man he'd reported for abusing a child. He'd told himself he had to stay calm and in control to make a good impression on the judge. But he couldn't help himself. The compulsion to turn his head was overpowering.

He didn't know what he'd expected. Some kind of monster, for sure. Something subhuman. He hadn't expected a perfectly ordinary-looking couple, just a couple you might run into in the supermarket, or at a PTA meeting. The man was dark, with curly hair and a receding hairline and a moustache. He wasn't a big man, but he looked fit. The woman had light brown hair cut short. She seemed nondescript, and wore a scared look that Zack thought was probably permanent. She kept looking around as if she expected something awful to pop out at her any minute. *Her* he could feel sorry for.

He turned back to face the judge's bench, but he

wasn't seeing it. He kept seeing Theresa's face, all bruised and swollen, with that one red eye. And then, without warning, he saw something he'd thought he'd managed to banish from his memory: Josh's face, as it had looked when he'd carried him out of the pool. And then the two faces, overlaying each other . . .

"Zack. Are you okay?"

It was Maddy's voice, tight with concern. Her hand was on his knee. He stared at her like a person waking from a nightmare. He wanted to say something to her, to reassure her, but at that moment the bailiff intoned, "All rise . . ."

The present reclaimed him; the hearing had begun.

"Now, that wasn't so bad, was it?" Larry asked. His grin was disgustingly cheerful, but his eyes were kind, and Zack knew he meant to be soothing.

They were back in the courtyard again, basking in welcome sunshine beside the Spanish fountain. Zack scowled at the merrily tumbling water, forgetting he'd ever touted its tranquilizing properties. "Still think you should have pressed charges," he grumbled. "That guy should be put away."

"So his wife can go on welfare?" Larry said mildly. "And the guy comes out angrier and more violent than when he went in?" His eyebrows lifted reproachfully. "Are you interested in justice or revenge, my friend? We've got the child. He'll never harm her again."

"*Temporarily.*"

"Oh, well, that's just procedure. The permanent-custody hearing's been set—"

"For July seventh. That's only thirty days." Zack shot a look of appeal at Maddy, who seemed to be avoiding his eyes. Either that or she'd developed a sudden fascination with Spanish tile. "That doesn't seem like very much time."

"It's a little shorter than usual," Larry said, "but that's because the aunt testified that there aren't any other relatives willing and able to take in a child. The court just needs enough time to verify that fact—they don't want her in limbo any longer than necessary—and then . . ." Larry beamed. "Theresa's ours."

"*Mine,*" Zack corrected him, glowering.

Larry's smile vanished. "Don't get your hopes up," he cautioned, looking grave and Lincolnesque. "As I've told you, you've either got to go talk to those people—the Sotos—and get them to agree to a private arrangement, or apply through the county. And as a single male parent . . ." He shrugged. "There's a long waiting list of couples ahead of you. Some of them have been waiting for years."

"Yeah, I know." Zack was frowning at Maddy, who was still steadfastly refusing to look at him. Dammit, what was wrong with her? She *had* to know he was trying to catch her eye!

"Where is Theresa now?" he asked softly, stubbornly keeping his gaze on Maddy's averted face.

Larry, with the kind of perceptiveness that made him such a good therapist, remained silent, so Maddy had no choice but to answer. Zack saw her shoulders rise and fall with a deeply drawn breath, as if she needed to fortify herself in order to talk to him.

"She's with a foster family," she said. "A really super family, named Frownfelter." She smiled, and added softly, "When I went to pick her up for the meeting with the judge, she was up to her elbows in peanut-butter-cookie dough."

Larry chuckled, but Zack refused to be sidetracked.

"Where is she now? How is she getting home?"

"Mr. Frownfelter picked her up and took her back. It was his lunch hour. . . ."

Her voice trailed off. It was odd, he thought. First she hadn't seemed to want to look at him at all, and now that he'd established eye contact with her, she couldn't seem to break it. Matter of fact, neither could he.

Not that he wanted to. She had such *nice* eyes. Gray, rather than blue, which he decided he liked better, because they were softer. And she had very dark lashes for someone as blond as she. Of course, he knew very well that for the price of a bottle of mascara anyone could have dark eyelashes, but hers seemed too soft and too thick to be anything but real. As a matter of fact, now that he thought about it, he didn't think she put much of anything on her face. Her skin . . . She had really nice skin, and like everything else about her, it made him imagine how it would feel against his own.

"Well . . ." Larry's cough was meant to be discreet, and sounded amused. "Time to get back to work. Maddy, can I give you a ride back to the clinic?"

Maddy actually shook herself, like someone trying to wake up. "Oh. No, thanks anyway, Larry. I have my car here."

"Right. Forgot. Okay, see you back at the ranch. And you hang in there, Zack. Patience, remember." Larry went loping across the courtyard toward the parking lot. Maddy turned as if to follow, but Zack put a hand on her arm.

"See you tonight?" he asked.

"What?" She seemed flustered. It gave her a nice touch of pink across the cheekbones.

"Your next swimming lesson." His voice felt furry in his throat. "This evening, same time, same station— right?"

"Oh. Right." She cleared her throat nervously. Good grief, he thought. Was she still afraid of him? "I'll see you later, I guess. . . ."

"Yeah, you will."

"Okay then, 'bye."

" 'Bye."

Scintillating conversations they had, the two of them, Zack thought sourly as he watched her make her way carefully across the courtyard's uneven tile paving. It frustrated him that he wasn't getting to know her as fast as he wanted to. He'd thought if he could just get her away from her puppets . . .

It occurred to him that Theresa might have somehow gotten in the way. He didn't know why, but ever since last night, something had definitely come between him and Maddy.

Theresa. Thirty days. Damn! He had just thirty days in which to find the stomach and the self-control to go to those people—the Sotos—and persuade them to relinquish custody directly to him. Either that, he thought with amusement, or he had thirty days in which to get married and move himself up in the county adoption board's eligibility ratings.

A short, ironic laugh escaped him. The only woman he'd even thought of in those terms in two years was just escaping around a hibiscus hedge, dashing for the parking lot for all the world as if she were escaping from *him*. He had a feeling it would take a lot more than thirty days to bring her around to thinking along the same lines!

It sure looked as if his best bet were the aunt and uncle.

"Hey! *You.*"

Zack looked around and muttered, "Speak of the devil," under his breath. Theresa's uncle was bulldozing his way across the courtyard toward him, with his wife clinging to his arm like a sea anchor.

"You're the guy from the pool, aren't you?" Soto said. "The swimming teacher." He managed to make the identification sound like an insult.

"Yes, I am," Zack said, proud of his calm. "And as a matter of fact, I'd like to talk to you. It's about—"

"Well, buddy, I've got a few things I'd like to say to you too. You're the guy who started this whole thing, aren't you?"

"Joe—"

"Shut up, Carleen!"

The man had shaken his wife off and was facing Zack across a few feet of tiled courtyard. His face was dark and angry, and his arms hung at his sides at the ready, like a gunfighter's.

Zack knew very well that at this point, discretion dictated a strategic withdrawal. So what did he do? He folded his arms across his chest and said very politely, "I reported it, if that's what you are making reference to."

"Look, I don't know who the hell you think you are, butting into a man's private business. I got a right to discipline a kid who smart-mouths me in my own home, you got that? You made a lot of trouble for me, you know that? I got cops hassling me, I could lose my job . . . Hey, I really oughta let you have it!"

"*Joe!*"

"Oh, now, I don't think you'd do that," Zack drawled. "I'm not a little kid."

He'd almost expected it. Hell, he'd probably invited it. But it was a shock to him anyway. He hadn't been hit in anger since fourth grade, when a kid named Hank Plunkett had bloodied his nose and given him a fat lip with one punch. It had come as a shock to him then, too, and he'd reacted reflexively. His instinctive response had left poor old Hank sitting in a puddle of water, clutching his middle and gasping like a netted fish. At that point Zack had touched his face, discovered blood, and had run for home, howling his head off.

It was interesting to discover how little had changed in twenty years.

His reflexes were still good, and his instincts for self-defense about the same. This time his assailant wound up in a fountain rather than a rain puddle, but his posture and facial expression reminded Zack a lot of Hank Plunkett. So did the sounds he was making.

At that point Zack touched his own lip, discovered blood, and decided it was time he headed on home.

The only difference twenty years made, as far as he could see, was that he wasn't howling his head off.

He did stop to mutter an apology to Theresa's aunt, who was standing frozen with shock, her mouth hanging open. He felt genuinely sorry for her. She had a tough time ahead of her if she stayed with that guy.

As Zack walked to his car he wasn't feeling particularly proud of himself, but he wasn't ashamed, either. He told himself he hadn't been spoiling for a fight, and in fact had behaved with remarkable restraint. He just couldn't decide whether he was glad or sorry Maddy hadn't been there to see it.

Then it occurred to him. *Damn!* he thought. There went his chance for a private deal!

He gave a sardonic laugh that hurt his swelling lip, winced, and muttered, "Ouch!" And he thought, *I guess this means I'll have to get married after all. . . .*

Zack didn't really mean that. Even if Maddy—or any other woman—had been willing, he'd never have done a thing like that to her. As far as he was concerned, there was only one good reason to marry, and that was love. He'd loved Carol, and she'd loved him, and they'd both loved Josh. He'd never marry again unless he could give that kind of wholehearted, unselfish love. A woman had a *right* to expect that much.

He knew why Larry Whitlaw had asked how long it had been since Carol's accident. The psychologist was telling him it was high time he stopped mourning and got on with his life. The thing was, he didn't *feel* as if he were still mourning, and he had an idea his life was moving right along whether he was ready for it to do so or not. Just because he wasn't actively looking for someone didn't mean he was avoiding relationships. When and if the right person came along, he was pretty sure he'd know it.

Just as he'd known that Theresa was the child for him. Not to take Josh's place—you couldn't ever replace one child with another. Kids weren't interchangeable. Until that day at the pool, when he'd squatted down in front of that tiny little girl and come face to face with those dark saucer eyes, he hadn't even realized how much he'd missed having somebody to love. Somebody who really needed him. When he met the woman he could love, maybe not exactly the same way he'd loved Carol but at least as deeply, he'd recognize her too.

He had a sudden, discomfitting vision, a memory, that was as clear as a video-taped replay: a pair of long legs, not deeply tanned, but creamy smooth; an absolutely spectacular body that looked as if it had been dipped in India ink; a face so frozen, it had lost all expression, except for the fear in the eyes . . .

It struck him that it would really be funny, wouldn't it, if it turned out he'd found both loves in the same moment?

Dahlia looked up suspiciously as he invaded her kitchen in search of a snack. "What are you grinning about, Zachary?" she asked.

With maturity and originality he singsonged, "I'll never tell." Still grinning, he snagged a handful of the cheese she was grating into a bowl and deftly evaded her attempt to slap his hand. "What's this for?"

"Dinner," Dahlia muttered darkly, "unless you stick that hand in here again, in which case you're going to be *wearing* it."

"Hmm. What's for dinner?"

"Why are you asking?"

He leaned against the counter and nibbled cheese with studied nonchalance. "Just wondered. Maddy's coming for a lesson after a while. Thought I'd ask her to stay for dinner, if there's going to be plenty. . . ."

Dahlia threw him a look. "It's lasagne. And you

know I always make enough for an army." She went back to grating cheese. "Pretty girl," she said with a sniff, giving him a sidelong glance.

"Who? Maddy?" His expression, he hoped, was one of complete innocence.

"Don't 'Who? Maddy?' *me*, Zachary London." Dahlia lifted an elbow in a halfhearted effort to dodge the kiss he planted on her cheek, and threatened to break into a smile. The smile vanished as she got a close look at him. "*Zachary!* What happened to your face? Son, what did you do?"

"Oops," Zack muttered, and put his hand over his mouth—too late. "It's nothing. Ran into a door."

"Sure, and I'm Snow White! Come here and let me look at you!"

"Come on, Dahl—"

"I said come on over here! You've been in a fight!" She put her hands on his shoulders and peered sternly into his face. "Don't you lie to me, Zachary. I raised five boys. I know a fat lip when I see one!"

"Would I lie?" Zack mumbled without conviction.

"Humph. Door, my eye! What you ran into was a *fist*. Now, you tell me who hit you, and why!"

Zack chuckled, then winced. "What are you going to do, go get him? As a matter of fact, it was Theresa's uncle."

"Theresa's *uncle?* I'm surprised he'd take a chance on hitting anything that could hit 'im back. You *did* hit him back, didn't you?"

"Thought you didn't approve of fighting."

"For that man I'll make an exception. You better tell me you gave him what he had coming!"

"I put him in the courthouse fountain," Zack muttered darkly.

Dahlia nodded, as if it were no more than justice. "Get along out of here and let me get my dinner made. Maddy's welcome. And you go put something on that lip."

Zack went obediently to the bathroom first, decided

there wasn't much he could do about his lip, then went out to check on the pool chemicals. He tried to whistle, found it impossible to do with a fat lip, and switched to off-key humming. The gloom he'd felt earlier, during and after the hearing, had cleared away completely. So had most of the vague sense of shame he'd felt at having behaved so childishly, though he'd definitely decided punching somebody in the stomach was nothing to be proud of and was glad Maddy hadn't seen it. But in spite of all that, right now he couldn't remember having felt happier in ages.

With a small sense of shock, he realized it was because Maddy was coming.

He didn't know why that should shock him, so he leaned his arm across one knee and thought about it while pool water and chemicals dribbled out of the plastic pH tester onto his pants leg.

Of course he'd known he found her damned attractive physically. To put it bluntly, he wanted her so badly, he could taste it, and probably had ever since the day she'd fainted into his arms. And he'd already been honest enough with himself to admit that this whole swimming-lesson business was nothing more than a way to get her away from her puppets and into his bed. Not the noblest motive in the world, true, but nothing to be ashamed of, either. They were both over twenty-one, and if she liked the idea as much as he did, why not?

This thing with Theresa was confusing what should have been a simple matter of chemistry, that was the problem. It was fogging up his judgment. Since he'd become so obsessed with the idea of adopting that little girl, he'd been thinking of everything in terms of *her* needs, not his. If he wasn't careful, he'd be judging Maddy according to how she might fit into his plans for Theresa, and lose touch with his own feelings. He could overestimate his attraction to her just because he knew she was good with kids.

Put more bluntly, he'd actually been thinking—only half in jest—of marriage to a woman he barely knew, because he figured she'd be a good mother for Theresa, and would therefore make *him* more acceptable to the adoption board!

Zack blew a silent whistle and shook his head. The thing to do, he thought as he packed up the test kit and got to his feet, was to make darn sure that from now on he separated the two. Theresa was important to him, but she was only one part of his life. Maddy—or any other woman he might happen to be interested in—was another. He didn't know yet just how important Maddy was going to become to him, but he intended to give himself a chance to find out. Starting tonight.

He finished cleaning the pool, and even swept a few stray leaves off the deck before going back inside. The smell of baking lasagne was already beginning to drift down to the basement room. Zack paused to frown at the clutter on the coffee table. Sure didn't look very inviting, and not at all romantic. Dahlia wouldn't touch this room, and he didn't blame her. The housecleaning service gave it a good going-over once a week, and he wasn't a kid, that he should have to be picked up after.

He glanced at his watch. Maddy would be here any minute. He didn't have time to do much, but he did what he could, gathering up newspapers and stuffing them into the overflowing trash, putting all the magazines in the closet, where they cascaded into and over Carol's golf bag and onto the pile of towels and bathing suits on the floor. He gave the tabletop a hasty wipe with a sweatshirt he found behind a couch cushion, and stood back to survey the setting dubiously.

Should he light a fire in the fireplace? It was June—might seem too obvious. On the other hand, they'd both be wet when they got out of the pool, and June nights were always cool. What the heck. They'd both appreciate a nice fire.

That done, he thought maybe he ought to put some place mats or something on the coffee table. Open a bottle of wine. Find some candles.

Now, that *would* be too obvious. But it made a seductive picture in his imagination, firelight and candle glow shining in soft gray eyes and even softer hair. Full lips, tasting of wine . . .

Zack grinned at his own erotic fantasies. He was really getting into this! And finding it fun, after so long in emotional hibernation. Exciting, and stimulating in ways he'd almost forgotten.

He actually jumped when he heard the doorbell. Shouting, "I'll get it, Dahl," he went bounding up the stairs, feeling younger and lighter than he had in years. When he opened the door he was already smiling.

It took him a couple of beats to realize that Maddy wasn't alone. He was focused on her, and her eyes were so luminous, her smile so shy, but somehow full of anticipation, as if she had a wonderful surprise for him.

And boy, did she ever. Clinging to Maddy's hand and gazing solemnly up at him with those saucer eyes of hers was Theresa.

Seven

Maddy wasn't sure why, at the last minute, she'd decided to ask Dottie Frownfelter if she could take Theresa with her to Zack's. It had just been one of those impulses she had so often and wound up regretting. She'd thought it would make Zack happy. Now she thought maybe it would have been better if she'd called first.

Zack's face was going through such a fascinating and puzzling series of expressions. Maddy spent a lot of time studying facial expressions, learning how to duplicate them in felt and fur and papier-mâché, and she knew very well that people's faces weren't always accurate barometers of their emotions. If she thought she saw disappointment on Zack's, she was probably just misreading him. She didn't seem to have much luck reading him anyway. And she knew he was crazy about Theresa. This afternoon he'd been disappointed and frustrated to the point of churlishness at not being allowed to see her. How could he possibly be disappointed?

He was just surprised, that was all. She really should have called first.

She took a deep breath, smiled, and opened her mouth to say "Hi." Instead she stopped, blinked, and blurted out, "What in the world happened to you? Your lip . . ."

Beside her, Theresa leaned against her leg and lifted her hand in a shy wave. Zack glanced down at her, then touched his lip gingerly and muttered, "It's nothing, Maddy. Ran into a door. Hey, Theresa! Nice to see you, squirt." If he had been disappointed, he'd made a quick recovery, Maddy thought. He gently touched Theresa's hair, and the pleasure on his face was unmistakable. "You been working on that kick like I told you? Nice, straight legs?"

Theresa slowly shook her head.

Zack looked stern. "Why not?"

" 'Cause I don't have a pool." Theresa shrugged matter-of-factly, secure in the knowledge that her excuse was irrefutable.

Zack looked shocked. "No kiddin'? Well, guess what? I do. Did you bring your bathing suit?"

Theresa proudly held up a small plastic purse with a picture of a Cabbage Patch doll on it. "Yep, it's in my purse—just like Maddy's! And you know what? Maddy even bought me this purse."

Zack looked at Maddy. She sucked in her breath at the look in the smoky blue depths of his eyes, then laughed and lifted her shoulders. "I thought you'd like to see her, after this morning. I hope . . . I know I should have asked. . . ."

"No. Hey, it's great! Come on in. Uh . . . Maddy, you know where to change. You can show Theresa—"

"I can dress myself," Theresa informed him loftily. "But somebody has to tie me."

"I'll help you, sweetheart," Maddy murmured.

Zack seemed about to say something, then rubbed a hand over his hair and gave a little cough. "Okay.

Well, then. Oh, wait." He raised his voice and bellowed, "Dahl!"

Maddy wondered if Zack's housekeeper had been listening from the kitchen doorway, because she appeared immediately, and didn't look the least bit surprised to see Theresa.

"Dahlia," Zack said, clearing his throat. "This is Theresa."

"Hello, Theresa." Dahlia's manner was warm, and, though no less queenly than usual, seemed to have softened indefinably. Maybe it was her voice, Maddy mused, still rich and mellow, but a little lighter, like an oboe played pianissimo. "I am so pleased to meet you."

"Theresa, this is Dahlia."

Theresa's head swiveled from Dahlia to Zack. In a loud whisper she asked, "Is she your mother?"

Maddy stifled a squeak and looked at Dahlia, who was trying to control her smile. Zack laughed and said, "No, she's not my mother. But she does take care of me."

Theresa nodded solemnly. This was something she could understand. "I don't have a mother either. But Dottie's taking care of me now. She lets me make cookies. I got to mash 'em with a fork!"

Zack looked at Maddy with raised eyebrows and mouthed, "I thought she was shy!" He seemed slightly dazed. Maddy laughed silently and shook her head. She'd been discovering that, freed from the fear of violence, Theresa could be quite a little character. In fact she could probably, as Maddy's father would have put it, "talk the hind leg off a mule."

"Well," Dahlia said, looking impressed and a bit dazed herself. "I'm fixing supper right this minute. Would you like to help me make the salad?"

"Are we going to stay for supper?" Theresa asked, tipping her head back to look at Maddy. Maddy looked at Zack, who nodded. "What are we having for supper? I smell something *good.*"

"Lasagne," Zack and Dahlia said together.

"Oh, I *love* lasagne! But I can't help make the salad." Theresa shook her head sadly.

"Why not, baby?" Dahlia looked gravely disappointed. Zack shrugged and looked at Maddy, who shrugged back.

" 'Cause Zack says I have to practice my kick."

"Tell you what," Zack said, dropping a hand to Theresa's shoulder. "I bet Dahlia wouldn't mind if you came and swam for a little while, and *then* helped with the salad."

"That would be good," Theresa said, nodding judiciously.

"That's fine," Dahlia agreed.

"Okay, squirt—scoot. Go get your suit on." As Maddy turned Theresa toward the hallway, Zack said in an undertone to Dahlia, "Give us fifteen minutes, then come and get her. And Dahl . . . thanks!" He dropped a quick kiss on the housekeeper's cheek and bounded down the stairs to the basement. Dahlia gave Maddy an enigmatic look and turned back to the kitchen.

Thanks? Maddy wondered. What for? For being nice to Theresa? For keeping her occupied? For fixing dinner? What? There were undercurrents here she didn't understand! She was still frowning over it as she took Theresa's hand and turned down the hall to the bathroom. Theresa, oblivious to undercurrents, was experimentally chanting, "Squirt, scoot, suit . . . Squoot, sirt . . . Hey, that's a *tongue twister!*"

He was so wonderful with her, Maddy thought as she sat in a deck chair and watched Zack work with Theresa in the shallow end of the pool. Really wonderful . . .

He used the same firm, no-nonsense approach Maddy remembered from that day at the public pool, but there was no comparing this Theresa with the frail creature who had clung so timidly to Maddy's hand and flinched in fear from Zack's touch. Maddy couldn't believe how far the girl had come in so little time. It seemed nothing short of miraculous to her to watch that tiny child fling herself off the side of the pool and into the water without a moment's hesitation, then kick to the surface and strike out with confidence for the side.

Maddy wondered if *she* would ever be able to come up out of the water the way Theresa did, laughing as she pushed streaming hair out of her face.

Now Zack had abandoned his teacher's role and was romping with Theresa like a playful dolphin. Sometimes he seemed to play so roughly that Maddy gasped and had to cover her eyes, but Theresa's shrieks and yelps were of joy and excitement, not fear. And Maddy noticed that whether Zack was tossing her into the air or ducking her in the water, his hands were always gentle, strong, and sure.

She trusts him, Maddy thought, remembering the way those firm and gentle hands had held *her* that day at the pool, remembering his voice in her ear saying, "You can do it."

She had trusted him, too, enough to put her face into the water. It was only when he let her go, she realized now, that she'd fainted.

She watched Zack take Theresa to the deep end of the pool on his back, knifing through the water with a powerful breaststroke, while Theresa giggled ecstatically and clung to his neck. And she remembered vividly the way that powerful body had aligned itself under hers, his chest muscles sliding against her back, the way her legs had tangled unexpectedly with his. . . .

Something flip-flopped inside her. She folded her arms across her waist and leaned over, pressing tightly against a hollow, quivery feeling in her stomach.

"Hey, what's the matter? Butterflies?" Zack was

standing there dripping and grinning, wiping his face with a towel.

Theresa peered at her around Zack's legs, black eyes sparkling above the folds of her own towel as she announced, "I had *fun!* Did you see me swim? Pretty soon I can go off the diving board. Zack says so!"

"Not so fast, squirt. Not until I tell you you can, and not unless I'm right there, understand?"

"Okay," Theresa muttered reluctantly. She recovered her bounce and sparkle when she saw Dahlia coming toward her with outstretched hands. "Oh, boy. Now we get to make salad! Hi, Dahlia! What do *I* get to do?"

"First of all, you get to get yourself out of those wet things," Dahlia said firmly. With a glance at Maddy and a nod toward Zack, the housekeeper took Theresa by the hand and led her, hopping and skipping in anticipation, into the house.

Zack, watching them go, shook his head and murmured, "What a difference." He turned to Maddy, who was still holding her stomach together. "You really have butterflies about this."

She shook her head—a silent lie. Actually, the butterflies were worse than ever. Oh, not the cold, sick kind. She hadn't felt those in ages. These were the hot, quivery kind she was coming to associate with only one thing: Zack's nearness.

What now? she wondered.

Zack was looking at her as if he were thinking the same thing. Then he held out his hand and said sternly, "Come on, Amanda. Your turn."

"Aren't we going in the hot tub first?" she asked plaintively as he pulled her out of the deck chair.

"Uh-uh. Not this time." He gave her a little half-smile that was warm with sensual memories. "Can't let you get too spoiled. Come on." He jumped into the water and patted the brick coping. "Sit down."

Maddy reluctantly obeyed, lowering her feet gingerly into the water.

Zack stepped close to her. The hard muscles of his belly bumped her knees. She caught her lower lip between her teeth and looked into his face, then couldn't restrain a tiny gasp as she felt his hands on her waist.

"Take it easy," he said, sounding irritated. "I'm not going to hurt you. Put your hands on my shoulders and jump down." When she hesitated, he snapped, "Come on, you can see the water isn't even waist deep."

Now he was angry with her, she thought, and wished she knew why.

All at once she felt depressed, utterly mired in wretchedness. She pressed her lips together as she placed her hands on Zack's broad shoulders. She focused on the off-center dimple in his chin to take her mind off the feel of that warm, resilient muscle beneath her palms . . . and the pressure of his hands on her body.

"Now," he said when she was standing in the waist-deep water, trying not to shiver, "follow me."

Not that she had any choice—his hands were still holding her waist. Her fingers clutched the hard, wet muscle of his shoulders as he pulled her slowly into deeper water. She could feel his gaze on her face and knew without looking that he was frowning. She kept her own gaze steadfastly glued to his chin, because she didn't dare meet his eyes. If she looked up, if she tilted her head just a little, her face would be only inches away from his. She could feel the cool stirring of his breath on her damp forehead.

The water swirled around her like the cool kiss of fine silk. When it touched her chest, Zack stopped and said, "Now, Maddy, I want you to bend your knees and let the water come right up to your chin."

Her knees turned to rubber. She couldn't make them obey. "Zack—"

"Come on, Maddy. *Do it.*" His voice was hard and uncompromising, but the pressure of his hands on her waist remained constant. He wouldn't force her, she knew that, yet she felt compelled nonetheless. She closed her eyes and lowered herself until the water lapped at her chin.

"Good girl . . ." Zack's voice became a reassuring drone. "Now close your mouth and let the water cover your lips. Just your lips. Keep your mouth closed, now. . . ."

Maddy tried. She really did try. She closed her mouth and tried to pretend the water was something else. Cloth . . . flower petals . . . But the images wouldn't stay put. They kept breaking up into green, slimy blackness. The tension under her ribs rose into her throat, strangling her, choking the life out of her. . . .

"No!" She erupted from the water with a cry of pure terror. "No. I can't!" She turned, groping wildly for the edge of the pool.

Zack's arms imprisoned her, coming around her from behind to prevent her escape. Hard arms, holding her tightly, just holding her, while she struggled and fought him with blind futility. He didn't try to speak until she had relaxed against him, limp and defeated. Then he said in quiet triumph, "That's it, isn't it? It's just your *face.* You can't stand the water on your face. Babe, don't you know how natural that is? Almost everybody hates putting his face in the water at first, but after you've done it a few times and you find out it isn't going to kill you, it isn't nearly as bad as you thought. Then—"

"But it's *worse!*" Maddy cried. Her head fell back onto his shoulder. She felt sobs tumbling through her and pressed her lips tightly together, hoping to hold them back. "Don't you understand? It isn't like that. It's always worse—worse than I can imagine!"

"Worse? Maddy, what do you mean? Tell me." His voice, like his embrace, was hard, rough, commanding. She shook her head frantically. One of those sobs managed to get away from her, but because she wasn't used to losing control at all, it came out a strangled whimper.

Zack's sigh lifted his chest against her back. Frustration showed in the barely controlled tension in his voice and his hands. "Okay, that's it. Enough for today. Come on."

He walked her to the steps and held her arm while she climbed out of the pool. She stood with her shoulders hunched while he reached for a towel, feeling terrible, like a wretched, miserable failure. Why couldn't she control her reactions, like an adult? Why couldn't she master her childish fears? Why was she such a weak, spineless *jellyfish?*

"I'm sorry," she said tightly, ignoring the towel he handed her and hugging herself instead. "I tried. I'm sorry. I know you're angry."

"Maddy—" She could see him take a deep breath and fight for patience. "Maddy, I'm not angry with you."

"Yes, you are."

"Okay, all right, I'm angry. But not because you can't put your face in the water. Dammit, it's because you won't *talk* to me about it, don't you understand? I can't help you if you won't talk to me!"

With unexpected gentleness, he draped the towel around her shoulders and used the ends of it to pull her closer. Maddy's heart began to hurl itself against her ribs. She stared doggedly at the drops of water that had collected in the hollow above his collarbone as he leaned forward and touched her forehead with his lips.

She pressed her lips together and sniffled. "Hey," Zack said, and lifted her chin with a knuckle. "Don't do that. I told you, we're going to beat this thing. You're my personal challenge, babe. If you think you're going to get off this easy, I'd better warn you—I don't give up. You don't get to the Olympics without a pretty good-sized helping of pure, bullheaded stubbornness!"

Maddy still wasn't trusting herself to look at his face, but she heard the smile in his voice and answered it with an unsteady laugh. "I can imagine."

"Yeah . . ." He gave her a little shake, and this time when he spoke she heard the iron in his voice. "So the next time you come, you make up your mind before you do about two things. One, that you trust me; and two, that you're here to *work*. Understand? Because I mean to get to the bottom of this thing."

She shivered, and finally lifted her gaze to his face. Her breath caught in a tiny hiccup of wonder. She thought of hard, unyielding things, like stone and steel. She remembered television cameras zooming in tight on a swimmer on the starting platform, poised for the gun, eyes narrowed, jaw muscles clenching. She knew that this man, when he made up his mind to go after something, didn't give up until he'd won it . . . whether it was an Olympic gold medal, a world's record, a little girl, or a close-held secret.

She realized suddenly that, for all his gentleness and charm, Zack London was a very ruthless man.

"One other thing," he said. He was watching her through half-closed eyes. His arms lay heavy on her shoulders, his fingers loosely interlocked at the back of her neck. "Next time you come here for a lesson, Maddy . . . come alone."

That surprised her. "But I thought you'd be happy. I thought you were so crazy about Theresa, and so anxious to see her—"

"I am crazy about Theresa, and I was happy to see her tonight. But there's a time and a place for everything."

"I just thought—"

"A swimming lesson isn't recreation. It's work. And when I work, I *work*, and I expect you to do the same."

"I'm sorry," she whispered.

"And Maddy." His voice dropped, softened. Behind the veil of his gold-tipped lashes she could see a kind of glow that seemed to catch her up and hold her, so that it was impossible to look away. "When I want to be alone with a woman, I don't want a six-year-old audience, no matter how much I love her. Understand?"

She shook her head in fruitless denial.

"Sure, you do," he said, and lowered his mouth to hers.

For an instant Maddy felt his lips on hers, firm and warm and wonderful. Then he jerked his head back and muttered a muffled and chagrined, "*Ouch. Damn!*"

She touched her own lips with her fingertips, smothering a nervous giggle.

"Not a terribly auspicious beginning," Zack said. "You want to try that again?"

Quite suddenly Maddy knew there wasn't anything in the world she wanted more than to try that again. And if it went as well as she thought it might, again and again and . . . "Yes, please," she whispered, and tried a smile. "Carefully."

His mouth was all but touching hers. "Carefully," he breathed, and slowly closed the gap.

Maddy had suspected it might be wonderful, but she could never have imagined anything like that kiss. It wasn't what she was used to. Men always seemed to want to . . . *push* so, to establish dominance right off the bat, she supposed, because they weren't sure enough of themselves. Their mouths were invariably hot and open, tongues unpleasantly intrusive. She found the whole thing so dismal, she'd all but stopped dating because of it.

Of course, Zack *was* hampered somewhat by a sore lip. But Maddy knew, she just knew, that the cut lip hadn't cramped his style in the slightest. . . .

There was nothing intrusive, or remotely unpleasant, about the way Zack's lips moved over hers. He seemed to take pleasure in the shape and texture of her mouth, as if it were a rare delicacy to be savored. Maddy stood very still, wrapped in wonder, lips parted and breath suspended, completely caught up in the feeling, the sensation of his mouth sliding over hers. And then unconsciously, she began to move her lips, too, tasting and savoring him as he did her.

She felt his tongue touch the parted edges of her mouth—not intruding, but just *there*, a natural part of him. It seemed a natural thing to touch it with her own tongue. . . .

It became more than wonderful. It began to be *fun*. Maddy felt a smile grow and blossom in the warm embrace of his mouth. Tiny effervescent shivers filled all her insides. She said "Mmm," and lifted a hand to touch the side of his face.

His arms came around her and drew her close. She opened her arms, and the towel, and felt their warm, wet bodies come together in what felt strangely like melting. She couldn't seem to tell where she left off and he began. That same melting-merging was happening, too, to their mouths. Somehow he was kissing her fully, deeply, and she couldn't have said how it happened or when it began. She only knew she never wanted it to end.

She didn't want it to end, but it did. A sound, deep and rich as a cello solo, entered her consciousness like the first tiny trickles of rain down a watershed. An instant later it was a torrent of awareness that broke over her like a flood. She pulled away from Zack and stood dazed and shaking, cold with shock.

"What—who is that?" Her jaws felt both tight and unhinged, if that were possible.

"That," Zack said dryly, "is why I'd rather you came alone next time."

"No, I mean—"

"I know what you mean." He had kept one hand on her shoulder, and was gently combing her hair back behind her ear with the other. Now he sighed and let that hand drop to her shoulder too. "It's Dahlia," he said with flat resignation. "Singing to Theresa, I imagine."

Dahlia's voice rolled out through the kitchen window, clear and full-throated. Maddy could feel— could almost *hear*—the slow rhythms of the gospel beat:

> Jesus . . . loves me,
> This I know. . . .

Maddy cleared her throat and laughed painfully, turning so that Zack's hands fell away from her shoulders. "My goodness, she's wonderful."

"Yeah," Zack said. He was watching her with that old, smoky look. "She used to be a gospel singer, years ago, before she was married. *I* think she could have been one of the great ones."

"She still could." Maddy shivered suddenly and violently, and pulled her towel around her.

"Sounds as though you know gospel music."

"I was raised on it," she said, shivering again.

"Let's go inside," Zack said abruptly. "There's a fire . . . you're getting cold." He dropped his arm across her shoulders.

Maddy didn't shrug his arm away—not quite. She just held her body rigid, refusing to allow herself to be drawn against him, no matter how much she wanted to. She remembered that warm melting together of their bodies, and missed it so much, she felt almost as if part of *her* were missing. She longed to get that feeling of oneness back again, but she knew it was impossible now. The moment had been destroyed by Dahlia's singing, as abruptly and totally as a bucket of ice water destroys sleep.

"Is Zack your boyfriend?" Theresa's question was off-hand, and accompanied by a monotonous snap-pop, snap-pop, as she fastened and unfastened the flap of her new purse.

Maddy threw her a startled glance. She was driving

Theresa back to her foster home through a late June twilight, and it was too dark in the car to see the girl's face. "No! Of course not. Where did you get that idea?"

"He was kissing you."

"Theresa!" Maddy laughed with embarrassment.

"Well, he was. I saw you."

"Oh."

"You know what? Vicki Frownfelter—she's my foster sister—*she* gots a boyfriend. She told me."

"Really? How old is Vicki?"

"Sixteen. She's ten years older than me," Theresa added proudly. "When I'm sixteen, will I have a boyfriend?"

"I'm sure you will, sweetheart." Maddy cleared her throat and said firmly, "But Zack is just a *friend* of mine. That's all."

Theresa shook her head and declared, "Uh-*uh*. That sure looked like a boyfriend kiss to me."

"Oh, yeah?" Maddy was laughing in spite of herself. "What makes you such an expert, young lady?"

"Not very much," Theresa admitted sorrowfully. "Whenever somebody kisses on television, Aunt Carly always turns the TV off."

"Well, Zack is not my boyfriend. I told you before. He's just . . . a friend."

Theresa heaved a huge sigh and leaned her head back against the car seat. "I wish Zack could be *my* boyfriend. But I'm too *little!*"

"You like him?" Maddy kept her voice casual.

"Oh, yes. Zack is really neat. I like Dahlia, too. She sings. The only thing is, she calls me 'baby.' But that's okay. I don't think she means it. Do you like Zack?"

"Theresa, I told you I do."

"No, you didn't. You just said he's your friend."

"You're going to make a great lawyer someday," Maddy muttered under her breath, beginning to see what Larry meant about being with a child outside the clinic and schools. "Yes, of course I like Zack!"

"Is that why you kissed him?"

"Theresa!"

"Well," she said obstinately, "you *were* kissing." The fastening on her purse began to pop-snap, pop-snap. . . .

Maddy glanced down at the stubbornly tilted head beside her and thought that Zack and Theresa were already a lot alike!

"Maddy—what the hell is this? Some kind of joke? Dahl said you called up and canceled your lesson! Dammit, you call me and explain."

Maddy winced at the frustrated fury that hissed from the message machine like blue flame from a welder's torch. Zack was upset, and she didn't really blame him. She wasn't sure herself what had made her cancel the lesson. She just knew she didn't feel ready for what might happen if she went back to Zack's place alone. Sensory memories had haunted her sleep, haunted her still. . . . The feel of Zack's hands on her waist, the cool firmness of his wet body beneath her hands, the taste and texture of his mouth, the roughness of his face rasping against her fingertips . . .

The butterfly feeling in her stomach seemed to have become a permanent condition.

She'd barely rewound the tape when the telephone rang shrilly. She started violently, then sat hunched and tense, waiting for the machine to pick up the call. She was almost certain she knew who it would be.

"Maddy—I know you're there." The angry voice confirmed her suspicion. "Larry said you'd gone home. I know you can hear me." There was a sigh. She could almost see him dragging a hand through his hair, fighting for control. A great, aching surge of emotion filled her, and she had to struggle against a compulsion to give in and pick up the receiver. Why was she resisting him . . . and her own desires?

"Come on, Maddy, why are you doing this? If you don't face up to this thing now, you never will. Dammit, don't hide from me!" And finally, a grimly muttered, "Okay, babe. This isn't the end of it!" A click, a beep, then silence.

Maddy sat for a moment longer, then picked up Bosley and slipped the dragon over her arm. She stared at the pink triangular face, and the dragon gazed back in silent reproach. For once, Maddy could think of nothing for either of them to say.

The phone rang again. She dumped Bosley hastily and rudely into her lap and reached for it, then snatched her hand back. It could be Zack again, hoping to catch her napping. He was persistent enough to try something like that. She waited tensely while the machine ran through her message. The beep sounded; then she heard a plaintive voice.

"Oh . . . Maddy, it's *Saturday.* Aren't you *ever* home?"

Chuckling with sheer relief, Maddy picked up the receiver and switched off the machine. "Hello, Jody, it's me."

"Oh! I'm so glad! I was beginning to think nobody alive ever answers a phone anymore. If you can't come, Amanda, I'll never forgive you. It's not my fault it's so spur-of-the-moment. I did try to reach you earlier." Jody paused to take a breath, and Maddy plunged into the breach.

"Don't you think you should tell me what I'll be missing if I can't come? And when I'd be missing it?"

"Oh. I guess that probably would be a good idea. Michael's finished his project! And we're all celebrating. Tonight."

"Project?"

"Yeah, that deck and fire pit he and Cliff have been working on *forever.* They've actually finished it, can you believe that? We were going to have a big thing

Fourth of July, but then we found out Mike is scheduled for the Tokyo layover, and since his flight this
weekend got canceled, we just decided to call everybody and do this instead. Nothing fancy, come as you
are. We aren't barbecuing. That's so suburban, and
anyway, who wants to stand around turning steaks
all night! So I've ordered some stuff from the deli. Cliff
wanted to break a bottle of champagne on the fire pit,
but Mike convinced him it would be a sinful waste of
good champagne, not to mention the damage it
might do to the fire pit, so we'll open the bottle the civ-
ilized way and christen the fire pit by burning the
cork with appropriate ceremony. So what do you
think? Can you make it? You *have* to come."

"Well . . ."

"Amanda, have you been running? Why do you
sound out of breath?"

"Gee whiz, I don't know Jody, you have that effect
on people sometimes! Okay, I'll come. What time?" It
had just occurred to her that Zack London was probably entirely capable of coming over here and hauling
her bodily to his place. But if she were safely away for
the evening . . .

"Oh, you know, seven-thirtyish."

"Oh," Maddy muttered, thinking fast. Her lessons
with Zack were scheduled for six. "How about if I
come over a little early and help?"

"By all means, come early, but not to help. Nobody's
doing anything much. It's just a casual little thing, no
big deal."

"Sure," Maddy said, laughing. Mike and Jody's parties were legendary, even beyond the limits of San
Ramon. "Okay, I'll be there. Is six too early?"

" 'Course not, darlin'. Bring your puppets—you can
keep the twins out of the buffet. Oh, I almost forgot.
Wear something sensational. I *might* have the most
marvelous surprise for you, if I can get—"

"I thought you said *casual*."

"Oh I *did*. It *is*. For everybody but you. Trust me,

Amanda. Okay, see you tonight. Gotta go. Lots of calls to make—"

Maddy laughed at the dial tone and hung up, shaking her head. "Something sensational," huh? she mused. What was Jody up to this time? Or more accurately, whom was Jody trying to set her up with this time? Whoever the poor guy was, she wondered if Jody had told him he was being "set up" or if it was going to be a complete surprise to him. Jody had worked it both ways. Maddy wasn't sure which was worse!

She picked up poor Bosley and began to smooth out her wrinkles. "Something sensational," she murmured thoughtfully as she adjusted the dragon on her arm. Why couldn't Jody just accept the fact that Maddy wasn't the "sensational" type!

"Honey," Bosley's Mae West voice crooned throatily, "it might just serve the lady right if you did show up in four-inch spikes and sequins."

Maddy laughed softly. She definitely wasn't in the mood to put up with one of Jody's efforts to pair her off with Mr. Wonderful. If it weren't for the possibility of Zack London's showing up on her doorstep breathing fire, she wouldn't even bother going to this party. Still, it might be fun to see Jody's unsuspecting male when Jody presented him to over six feet of blond Amazon. Poor thing might have a heart attack, which *would* teach Jody a lesson!

Maddy shook her head and hung Bosley back on her stand. What a terrible thing to think! She didn't know where such ideas were coming from. She was feeling very odd today—restless and reckless and out of step with herself. She sighed and looked at her watch. She'd never go as far as black sequins, but she did have time for a quick trip to the mall, and it had been a while since she'd bought a new dress, just for fun. And besides, it would get her out of the house, out of reach of the telephone. . . .

• • •

"Good *night*. Hel-lo *gorgeous!*" Mike Harbor was in his own doorway, looking as if he'd been standing behind a 747 when somebody started the engines.

Maddy blushed furiously. "Thanks a *lot*, Mike. I really need that."

"Darlin', you're the only person in the world who'd take that as an insult. Sorry. Lost my head." He tucked the hammer he'd been holding under one arm and held out his hand. Assembling his face into an attitude of comic gravity, he intoned, "Maddy, my dear, you're looking mah-velous. Do come in. You'll find Jody out by the pool, I think. Mind if I tag along? I'd just like to watch people's faces when they get a load of you in that dress."

She'd gone too far, Maddy thought in panic. Where did she get these impulses?

The dress was red, not black, and it had tiny white polka dots instead of sequins. It was an off-the-shoulder sundress with a tight bodice made of something stretchy, and a swirly skirt that came just below the knee. It was cut so low in front and back that she couldn't possibly have worn a bra with it, but it fit her like a leotard anyway, so it didn't matter. Her red sandals only had three-inch heels, which put her height at just over six feet, a little more if you counted hair, which she'd curled, for a change, then fastened back with combs so that the curls cascaded down her bare back. Her reckless mood had sustained her this far, but she was beginning to feel sanity coming on.

"Hey, everybody," Mike—the rat—bellowed as he ushered her onto the patio. "Look who's here!"

A hush fell. Mike and Jody's next-door neighbor, Cliff Dawson, was standing on a ladder, stringing a net of tiny lights. He sat down abruptly on the top step and stared at Maddy with his mouth open. His hammer clattered to the deck, and his wife, Lois, picked it up and hit him on the shin with it. He didn't even blink.

Mike gave Maddy a smug I-told-you-so grin and said, "Hah!"

Jody walked across the lawn toward her, beaming like a proud mother. "Amanda, that's *perfect*. Absolutely perfect. I didn't think you'd really do it, but let me tell you, you're going to be glad you did, I guarantee it. Wait till you see—no, no! Not there. That goes over *there!*" She dashed off to intercept two caterer's assistants loaded down with trays.

Maddy turned to Mike and muttered, "Where's that champagne? I think I need a drink." She was joking. She wasn't much of a drinker at any time, and Mike knew it.

"Sorry, no champagne until the grand opening. How 'bout a beer?"

"In this dress? Are you kidding? Where would I put it?"

Mike shook his head and breathed heavily. "Darlin', I do see your point."

Maddy was saved from having to think up a rebuttal to that as the Harbors' twin boys came clattering onto the patio, shouting in two-part harmony. "Maddy, Maddy, there you are! What took you so long? Mom said you were coming to play with us. Did you bring any puppets? Did you bring Bosley? Can I work him?"

"No, *I* get to work him!"

"It's *my* turn. You got to last time!"

"Did not!"

"Did too. It's *my* turn. Maddy!"

Maddy gazed down fondly at the two curly blond heads. The boys' cheeks were pink, their grins appealingly gap-toothed, their eyes wide. And they were totally unimpressed by the way she was dressed. Thank heaven for the kids. To them she was still just plain old Maddy, and that meant only one thing.

"Come *on*, Maddy—where are they? Which ones did you bring?"

She stared down at the two little boys now with a

sense of shock. For probably the first time in her life, she'd forgotten all about her puppets!

"Hey, guess what?" she said. She took one small hand firmly in each of hers and thought fast. "I'm going to show you guys how to make a puppet of your own. Who's got a sweat sock?"

"I have!" both boys shouted.

"Clean?"

They grinned and lifted their shoulders in identical shrugs.

Maddy spent two delightful hours sitting cross-legged in the middle of the twins' bedroom floor, her lap full of felt and paper scraps, her fingers collecting a layer of glue and paint. When she heard Jody calling from downstairs, she brushed herself off with reluctance, kissed the boys, and silenced their protests by promising to bring Bosley soon. Then, with a fatalistic sigh, she left the room to face Jody and her latest victim.

She was already halfway down the stairs before it struck her that the man with his arm in Jody's clutches looked terribly familiar.

Nobody else in the world could have hair like that.

She thought about turning around and escaping back up the stairs, but her legs weren't up to it. And besides, it was already too late. He'd seen her.

"Oh, Maddy, there you are," Jody said. "I should have known. Look who's here. Isn't it marvelous? I know you two have met."

"Yes," Zack murmured. "We have. Hello, Maddy."

Eight

Maddy managed to croak "Zack," but that was all.

He just stood there with his hands in his pockets, scowling up at her. Jody looked from his face to Maddy's and seemed to conclude that, though her surprise wasn't producing quite the reaction she'd intended, this was infinitely more interesting. And then, because for all her blithe and sometimes thoughtless nature she really wasn't an insensitive person, she apparently decided to leave things to percolate naturally.

"Oh, look," she cried suddenly, "there are the Duncans. I'll leave it to Maddy to show you around, Zachary. Excuse me. Hilary, how wonderful you look! What a marvelous tan! Tell me all about Mazatlan. . . ."

Her voice faded into background noise. Maddy cleared her throat. She couldn't think of anything to say, and Zack wasn't helping her out. Why was her throat so dry? Why did she have the feeling that if she let go of the banister, she'd sit down rather more abruptly than she would care to?

"Well," she said at last. "I didn't know you knew Jody."

"I didn't," he said shortly, "until this afternoon."

"Oh."

"I'm here because she told me you would be. I'm not very big on parties."

"Oh," Maddy said, and took a deep breath. She wished he'd stop looking at her like that. He hadn't even seemed to notice her dress. Like Jody's boys, he didn't seem to find anything at all unusual about the way she looked. To her surprise, Maddy began to feel vaguely miffed. Darn it, the one time she'd ever really *wanted* a man to think she looked nice, she might just as well have been wearing sweats!

She shrugged, and began, with dignity, to descend the stairs. The discovery that she'd left her shoes on the twins' bedroom floor made dignity a little more difficult to manage, but she held her head high and did the best she could. "Well," she said with a wave of her hand, "now you see why I couldn't come for my lesson tonight. I'd have explained, but—"

"Baloney."

"I beg your pardon?"

"I said, baloney. You left that message with Dahlia at nine o'clock this morning. Jody didn't even tell you about the party until this afternoon."

"How do you know?" Beyond miffed and well along toward anger, Maddy paused on the bottom step, where she would have a height advantage even without her three-inch heels.

Zack took care of that simply enough. He put his hands on her waist and lifted her down beside him. "Because when Jody called *me*, she told me she'd just finished talking to *you*."

Maddy opened her mouth, closed it again, and muttered, "Thanks a lot, Jody."

Zack's smile was grim. "Never pays to lie, Maddy."

She stared at him in helpless fury, then whirled

and stalked out to the patio. It was much harder to stalk impressively when barefoot.

The party had gotten well underway while she'd been hiding upstairs with the children. The christening ceremony had obviously already taken place, because there were glasses of champagne on the buffet tables, and the caterers were circulating with open bottles. Maddy snatched a plastic glass from the table and downed its contents in one gulp.

"Better take it easy," Zack murmured sardonically. "I think that stuff's supposed to be sipped, not gulped."

"You drink champagne your way," Maddy said furiously, "and I'll drink it *my* way." She didn't feel like telling him she wasn't accustomed to drinking champagne *any* way. Pointedly turning her back to him, she managed to snag a caterer with a bottle, and avidly watched him fill her glass to the brim.

"For your information," she informed Zack as she took a prim sip from her glass, "I was *thirsty*." She turned to pick up a second glass from the buffet table and waved it recklessly at him. "Here, have some."

He muttered, "No, thanks," and went on watching her through half-closed, shadowy eyes.

She shrugged, and took a sip from that glass to hide her fury. Who did he think he was, tracking her down like this, cornering her at her best friend's party? Just because she'd broken a little old appointment! He was acting as if he owned her! As if she owed him something! *He'd* offered to teach her to swim—she hadn't asked him! If she changed her mind, that was her business, not his! She didn't need him butting into her personal, private affairs. She didn't need him at all, and if she didn't want to tell him her life's story, that was her business too!

Inexplicably, the pressure in her chest surged up into her throat and threatened to escape in the form of humiliating tears. She ducked her head and desperately gulped champagne.

"Maddy . . ." Zack took the empty glass from her hand and set it on the table. When he tried to relieve her of the other glass as well, she eluded him, and muttered, "That's *mine*."

"Come on, Maddy."

Hah, she thought. He was beginning to sound frustrated. Good. He deserved it. He shouldn't have come here. It wasn't going to do any good. She wasn't going to get in that pool of his again. She wasn't going to go back to his place again, either. Not alone. Because if she did . . .

"Come on, that's enough champagne." He finally captured the now-empty glass and disposed of it, then caught her wrists.

She stared down at his hands, then said imperiously, "Let go, please."

He shook his head. "Not until you stop this nonsense and tell me why you bolted."

She stared at him, and wondered why her eyes had developed a tendency to cross. Maybe she needed glasses. "Bolted? What's that mean?"

"Why you quit—gave up—chickened out!"

"I didn't chicken out. I just . . ." She looked longingly at the champagne, but Zack was still holding her wrists. "I just . . ." She took a deep breath and frowned. If she started to cry here, in front of all these people, she'd never forgive him. Ever.

"Maddy, come with me. Now. Let's go back to my place and get to the bottom—"

"Can't go swimming," she declared. "I just curled my hair."

"No swimming. We'll just talk, okay? Just talk to me, Maddy. Tell me what's making you so afraid. Please."

She shook her head. She could be just as stubborn as he could. She wasn't even sure why she was being stubborn. She only knew that Zack London scared her more than the water did. He was demanding things of her that she wasn't sure she was ready to give. Making her feel things she wasn't ready to feel. If she went with him now, she'd have to confront those emotions, and she had a notion that once she did, her life would never be the same again.

Zack took a deep breath and muttered, "Okay, Maddy, that's it. I came here to get you, because we have some unfinished business. Now, are you going to come with me, or do I have to carry you out of here?"

"Hah!" she crowed triumphantly. "I'd like to see you try it. It's one of the advantages of being as big as me—as I . . . am."

"Yeah?" His smile had a dangerous twist. Maddy saw that look and thought, Uh-oh. She'd gone too far.

Zack let go of her wrists and put his hands on her waist, measuring it judiciously, and measuring with his eyes the parts of her his hands couldn't. Maddy felt those parts begin to tingle and ache. "Sorry to have to disillusion you," he drawled. "You're *tall*, not big. As a guess, I'd say you don't weigh more than . . . one thirty. I routinely press a whole lot more than that, sweetheart. And you're forgetting. I carried you once before."

"Oh, yeah?" Maddy said with champagne belligerence. "Kicking and screaming?"

He lifted his eyebrows. "Oh, would you kick and scream? It's okay with me if you do, but I wouldn't have thought you'd relish being the center of so much attention."

She considered that. She was beginning to feel a little funny and light-headed. Maybe it wouldn't be altogether *bad* to be carried. She had sun-shot visions of Snow White in the arms of Prince Charming. . . .

"Which will it be?" Zack asked stonily. "You can come with me on foot or over my shoulder."

She gazed at him in horror. "Are those the only two choices?"

He nodded. His jaw looked implacable.

She gulped, got a good grip on her pride, and said, "I believe I'll walk, thank you."

Zack's car was a Mercedes—one of the little two-seaters. Maddy wondered foggily how he could afford such a car, selling sporting goods. Then she remembered his house and Dahlia and the golf course, and muttered, "How come you told me you sell sporting goods?"

He snorted. "Because I do," he said, and opened the door to the passenger side. He waited while she got in, then slammed the door and went around to the other side. As he was getting in, she muttered something very witty about being kidnapped by Aquaman. He slammed his door and sat there looking at her without starting the motor.

"Maddy," he said finally, and dragged his hand through his hair. "Why are you being so childish about this?"

"I'm not childish!"

"All I want to do is help you accomplish what you set out to do in the first place, that day you showed up in my swimming class. Remember? But I can't help you if I can't get you to open up to me." His laugh was sharp and full of irony and frustration. "You know, it's really funny. You're acting just like those frightened kids you work with every day. Except you get through to them with your puppets, and I don't have anything to use to get through to you!"

"I'm *not*," she said in a tight, tense voice she didn't recognize. She suddenly felt cold and sick.

Zack had been staring out through the windshield. Now he slowly turned his head to look at her.

"I'm *not* like them. I'm not a child. And I've never been . . . been . . ."

"That's it, isn't it?" His voice was very soft. "I asked you if you'd been mistreated, and you denied it. But you're scared to death to talk about something that happened to you, something that happened when you were a child. I'd stake my life on it."

Maddy sat frozen, staring down at her clenched fists.

"You can't face it. You can't admit the fact that you were an abused—"

"I *wasn't!* I wasn't. My parents were just strict, that's all. I was their only child. They were very religious—they wouldn't *do* that. They *wouldn't*. They never harmed me. Never meant to harm me!"

"Maddy." Zack's hands, like his voice, were firm. He was holding her the way he'd held her that day in the pool. "Maddy, there's all kinds of abuse—you should know that better than anybody. There are all sorts of ways to harm a child. Some of the worst ways don't even show. Please . . . please tell me."

All of a sudden it seemed easier to tell him than to keep it all inside her. "He never meant to hurt me," she whispered. "He didn't—I know he didn't."

"I know," Zack murmured. "Tell me about it, Maddy."

"He only wanted me to learn how to swim. It was the way he'd learned. He took me to the pond . . . and he told me that all God's creatures were born knowing how to swim. It was natural. If I'd just let Him, God would take care of me. So he made me . . . he made me jump in the water. I tried, Zack. I tried to think about God. But there were *things* in the water. Moss, and slippery things that touched my legs. I guess I panicked, because I got water in my nose, and in my mouth, and then I couldn't keep . . . my head above the water. I couldn't breathe, and I couldn't see, and there was moss all over my face, and in my eyes, and . . . and—"

"It's all right, Maddy. It's okay." Zack's voice sounded ragged. "What finally happened?"

"I don't remember," she said dully. "Does it matter?"

"No," he breathed, and started the motor.

• • •

In those awful moments, listening to her talk, Zack had seen the child Maddy must have been: flaxen braids and soft gray eyes, and the endearing, long-legged awkwardness of a newborn colt. An exquisite and precious child.

Rage engulfed him—the same cold, overwhelming tide that had left him feeling so helpless and frustrated when he'd seen those bruises on Theresa's face. Dammit, *every* child was a rare and beautiful miracle. They were all supposed to be nourished and kept from harm, encouraged to grow and blossom. . . .

An old grief replaced the rage, taking him by surprise. It swept through him and then receded, leaving him feeling calm, but more vulnerable than he'd been in a long time.

He pulled into his own driveway, switched off the motor, and turned to look at Maddy. In the dim light he could see her throat move, but she didn't say anything. She hadn't said a word since he'd started the car.

He got out and shut his door, then went around to open hers. "Maddy? Come on, we're here."

She didn't move. In a thin, careful whisper she said, "I don't feel very well."

Zack swore softly. The streets of San Ramon Estates were winding, and he had been driving pretty much on automatic pilot. He wasn't used to having a passenger to worry about. Belatedly contrite, he took her arm and helped her out of the car.

"Take deep breaths," he instructed her tersely. "And *walk*. Dammit, why didn't you tell me you were carsick? And you had all that champagne. Did you eat anything?"

She looked appalled at the very thought.

Muttering profanely under his breath, Zack slipped his arm around her waist and walked her to the front door. She leaned against the door while he tried it, then unlocked it. When he pushed it open he had to grab her to keep her from falling through. At least the locked door meant that Dahlia had already left, thank heaven. She usually spent Saturday nights at her sister's, so they could go to church together early in the morning.

"All right, Maddy, in you go. Do you want to lie down?" She shook her head. He frowned at her, feeling helpless. "You need something in your stomach besides champagne. You go lie down while I fix you something to eat. Some of that lasagne, maybe—"

Maddy's eyes got round and dark. Suddenly she clapped a hand over her mouth and bolted for the bathroom.

Zack uttered a short, ugly word and raked a hand through his hair. He was furious with himself, and with his own impatience. He hadn't meant to do this to her. He'd only meant—had really wanted—to help her. Where along the way had his desires become more important than her problems? His need to know more important than her feelings?

He was a rat, and he wouldn't blame her if she never spoke to him again.

With a sigh of pure frustration, he threw up his hands and stalked into the kitchen.

She came in while he was making toast. She looked pale and chastened, and a few wisps of hair had escaped the combs and were clinging damply to her face.

"Did you throw up?" he asked bluntly.

She nodded.

"You're better off without that champagne in your system."

She nodded again and cleared her throat. "I didn't have that much. Three glasses. I don't know—it must be nerves."

"Three glasses in about three minutes." Zack added two more slices of toast to the pile on the plate in front of him and put another batch in the toaster. "You probably aren't used to that much alcohol hitting you all at once—especially on an empty stomach."

"Actually," she said, sounding embarrassed, "I'm not really used to drinking at all. I don't know what got into me."

"Well," he muttered, scowling at the toaster. He knew very well what had got into her. "What you need is something to eat. I made you some tea and . . . uh . . ."

"Toast," Maddy supplied as the latest batch popped up.

"Yeah."

"Well, thanks."

"Don't mention it."

"Um . . . where's Dahlia?"

"At her sister's. She always spends Saturday night at her sister's."

"Oh . . . Zack? Don't you think that's enough toast?"

He stared down at the leaning tower of toast, then up at Maddy. Her cheeks were very pink, her eyes suspiciously bright. As he glared at her, her mouth began to quiver. She put a hand over it, but a snort of laughter bubbled up anyway. Something inside him that had been wound too tight slowly came unraveled, and he began to laugh silently, his body shaking with it. He carefully laid the butter knife down on the counter and turned around.

"Maddy," he said softly. "Come here."

He was a little surprised that she came so readily, and surprised, too, at the way she fit so well against him. It wasn't the first time he'd held her in his arms, of course, but then he hadn't really been noticing things like that. He'd been too wrapped up in his own desires.

Now, as he pulled her close, he felt the shape of her against his own body; the shape of *her*, not of breasts and belly and thighs. She trembled a little as her arms encircled him, and he felt the steady thumping of her heart against his chest. He held her very tightly for a few moments until the tension in her eased. They both shifted, adjusting the fit, settling closer to each other. Zack leaned back comfortably against the counter, pulling her with him, then touched his lips to her hair and whispered, "I'm sorry."

"It's okay. You were right—I was childish." She stirred restlessly, and he tightened his arms around her for a second or two.

"No, you're not childish. I shouldn't have said that."

"Well . . . whatever you call it. You were right, I couldn't face it. I didn't *know*, Zack." Her words came rapidly, as if she had to get it all said while she still had the nerve. "I didn't know until I started working at the Crisis Center. And then I didn't want to believe it—accept it. I *couldn't*." The anguish in her voice was raw and real. "They're my parents, Zack, the only family I have. They *love* me. I don't want to hate them. They really didn't know what they were doing to me. *I* didn't know, until I came to the clinic. I just thought it was me. That I'd been a bad kid . . ."

Zack just held her and let her talk, stroking her back in an idle, petting way, while her words put haunting pictures in his mind. *Amanda* . . . beautiful, fairy-princess child; older parents, stern, righteous, no-nonsense, and God-fearing. To them she must have seemed like a foundling child—the devil's foundling.

The miracle was, he supposed, that they'd done so little permanent damage. But then, he was discovering that kids could be remarkably resilient. Oh, yeah, Maddy was afraid of water, and even afraid of her own beauty. And she'd had to find a way to hide her natural sparkle from everybody—behind those puppets of hers. But fears could be overcome, with patience. Her beauty and sparkle were still there—that was the miracle. All she needed was for someone to make her believe it was okay, even wonderful, to be Amanda Gordon.

Zack knew quite suddenly that he wanted to be that person.

". . . I thought it was bad, somehow, being pretty," Maddy was saying.

He leaned back so she could see his smile. "You don't still think so, do you?"

"No . . ." She touched her forehead to his chin, and he felt it crease as she struggled to understand and explain. "Not in my head. But in my heart—well, it's just . . . I don't like to be told I am, for instance. It never makes me feel good to be complimented on my looks, and I think it's supposed to. Sometimes I wish . . ."

"Wish what? That you looked different? Everybody probably wishes that at one time or another. But let me tell you what I believe, okay? Free of charge." This time he took her chin in his hand and tipped her face up, so he could look into her eyes. "You get what you get, period, and that's a gift. Rejecting it is like rejecting your gift."

She laughed. "Bad manners."

"Yeah, exactly. So the best you can do is accept your gift with style and grace and go on from there. You can make the most you can out of what you get, or you can just let it all go to pot." He grinned wryly. "Unfortunately, sooner or later, most people do let it go to pot—literally."

She pulled away from him and put her hand on his flat stomach. "You haven't," she observed, smiling.

It was an ingenuous move. He didn't think she had any idea what it would do to him. Getting a tight rein on his self-control, he put his hand over hers and kept it right there against his belly, a warm and intimate prisoner.

"No," he said, taking hold of her eyes as firmly as he had her hand, "I take good care of my gift. And so, obviously, in spite of everything, do you— No, Maddy. For Pete's sake, don't *flinch!*"

"Sorry," she mumbled. "It's a reflex."

He put his free hand on her neck, cradling her head, and gave her a little shake. *"Don't reject your gift!"* And then to his astonishment, he heard himself add, through tense jaws, ". . . like Carol did."

"Carol?" She was watching him intently now, a frown creasing the space between her eyebrows. "You mean your wife?"

He nodded. "Yeah. She was beautiful too. Worked as a model before we were married. She took good care of herself, until after we lost Josh. Then she quit caring. I couldn't make her care—nothing could. She tried everything she could to ruin what she had—ate, drank, you name it. And she finally succeeded, in spades. Ran her car into a telephone pole about a mile from here." Maddy's cheek felt cold in his palm. Her eyes were wide with horror, but Zack felt merely sad. It was all long past. There was no more horror left for him. Just a vast sadness, and a deep, lonely sense of regret.

Maddy licked her lips and asked, "Josh . . . was your son?"

"Yeah." He looked down at the soft place where her throat began and saw it move as she swallowed. He stared at that spot as if it were the most fascinating thing he'd ever seen.

"Please . . . tell me how it happened."

It didn't occur to him until later that she was asking him a question she'd never asked a living soul before without a puppet on her arm to buffer her from the pain in the answer. Her hands were at his waist, touching *him*, holding *him*. Her gaze was clinging to his. She was opening herself to him, and taking his pain into herself. . . .

"Maddy," he said. His throat felt raw. "It was just one of those things that happen. We were both there, and there wasn't anything either of us could do. He was riding his tricycle—Josh knew he wasn't supposed to ride his tricycle on the deck. But he . . . uh . . . rode his tricycle right into the pool. We didn't see it, so we can only suppose he was going too fast around and around, and couldn't make the corner. Anyway, he must have hit his head going in, and then was tangled up in the tricycle. Carol heard the splash—I pulled him out. We resuscitated him, but his lungs were full of water, and he was brain-injured besides. He died three days later."

Maddy was finally able to tear her gaze from him. It was drawn, against her will, toward the pool.

"We were living in Beverly Hills then," he said, and saw relief in her eyes as she looked back at him. "I bought this house because of Carol . . . hoping she'd start to take an interest in golf again—in *something*. You see, she never got over the guilt. We both blamed ourselves—people do, at times like that. We both saw counselors, together and separately. . . ." He shrugged. "With me it helped; with her it didn't."

Maddy whispered, "Zack," and put her arms around him. He took a huge breath and folded her into his arms, and again they just stood still for a time, holding each other. After a bit Zack chuckled, and blew a tickling wisp of her hair away from his nose.

"I guess this is what's called 'catharsis,' " he said.

She sniffed. "It's called 'getting rid of all the bad stuff at once.' "

"Right."

"Zack, I don't think I'll ever drink champagne again."

"Why? You're not sorry this happened, are you?" He tipped her face up again so he could see it.

"No."

"Me either. In fact, I'm damn glad."

"Me too." He looked at her for a moment longer; then he kissed her. Just a little kiss, a kiss of comfort and friendship.

At least . . . it started that way.

Her mouth was petal-soft, and tasted, rather surprisingly, of toothpaste. He felt her sigh as her arms lifted and wound around his neck.

It hit him then like a blast from a twelve-gauge shotgun, both barrels. One minute he was holding Amanda, person and friend. The next minute his arms were full of Maddy, the woman whose beauty had stirred him from the very first, and rekindled fires he'd thought dead. He felt the fullness of her breasts like brands against his chest, felt the sweet inward curve that brought her belly flat against his, felt the sliding pressure of her thighs aligning with his. There was a vast ache in his loins; a shudder ran through him; self-control fled. He groaned and dropped his arms low, pulling her hard into his body. His mouth found that soft place on her throat. Her body was all warmth and yielding softness. He heard her whisper something—his name?—as she threaded her fingers through his hair.

It was what he'd wanted, what he'd planned for. Maddy pliant and vulnerable in his arms, Maddy responding to his passion with nothing standing between them—not a little girl, not her puppets.

And he couldn't believe how stupid he'd been. Stupid to think he could ever have been satisfied with sex and nothing else. Stupid to think he'd be content to possess her body without knowing and treasuring *all* she was.

And he'd not only been incredibly stupid, he'd been arrogant. He'd been so certain he'd *know*, right away, like a light bulb coming on in his head, the way he'd known about wanting Theresa. Why hadn't he realized that loving a woman would be a whole lot more complicated than loving a child? More complicated . . . and too easy to confuse and mistake for other things . . .

Well, he'd wanted Maddy just where he had her right now. In fact, though it shamed him to admit it,

he'd maneuvered her here with the same concentra-
ted determination he'd always put into achieving anything he'd ever wanted. And now that he'd won, he
knew he couldn't do it to her. He wanted more from
her than a yielding body—a lot more.

The effort it took to control his desires left him
vibrating like a plucked string. His jaws felt as if
they'd been wired shut. He managed to grate out,
"Maddy," and pulled her arms from around his neck.

"Maddy," he said, praying she would understand, "I
think I'd better take you home now."

She wasn't going to understand. He could see it in
her eyes. They were glazed and dark with shock. He
held her hands together in both of his and said gently, "Believe me, I don't want to. But . . . you're very
vulnerable right now. We both are. You're a warm,
compassionate woman, and I've just unloaded on
you. We're holding on to each other for comfort.
Maddy, I can't let you get caught up in the moment
and do something you'll regret later."

She opened her mouth, then closed it. He saw her
throat move. She wouldn't argue with him—she
didn't have enough self-confidence for that—but he
knew she felt rejected. He hated doing this to her, but
the alternative was unthinkable. In a little while,
when she'd had a chance to recover her sanity, she'd
thank him.

"Come on, I'll take you home," he said, still struggling with his rigid jaws. He glanced down at her feet.
"Get your shoes."

She shook her head. "Don't have any. I left them at
Jody's. Just take me back there, please. I have to get
my car."

"Oh," he said. "Of course."

He drove her back to the Harbors' in silence. The
party was still in full swing. He sat in his car and
waited while she walked barefooted up the walk. He
knew he should have gone with her, but he didn't
think he could have faced her at the door, said good

night to her, without pulling her into his arms. He didn't think he had it in him to let her go twice in one night.

When she had disappeared through the Harbors' front door, he put his car in gear and drove slowly and carefully home. He let himself into his empty house and made straight for the basement. As he crossed the room he was pulling his shirt off over his head, kicking off his shoes, yanking at his belt buckle. By the time he reached the pool he was naked. Without missing a stride he launched himself through the air in a shallow racing dive. His body cut like a knife through the cool, silky blackness.

He thought it probable that anyone watching him enter the water must have heard the hiss of steam. . . .

He swam underwater until his chest began to feel like a bass drum, then surfaced and ploughed up and down the length of the pool until he was thoroughly winded. As he was dragging himself out of the water he thought he heard the chime of his front doorbell.

He froze, listening, while they pool water undulated, glittering with reflected moonlight. It came again, distant but unmistakable.

Damn, he thought. Who the hell could *that* be?

Muttering oaths under his breath, he found a towel and knotted it carelessly around his hips. Leaving a trail of wet footprints and water droplets, he ran up the stairs and strode to the door. Flung it open. And stood frozen with disbelief.

Maddy stood there, holding her shoes in one hand.

Nine

"I can't believe I let you do that," she said, breathing hard through her nose. She'd worked up a good head of steam on the drive there, and she was ready to let it blow.

Zack looked as if he'd run into a wall. He blinked at her and croaked, "What?"

"I can't believe I let you decide for *me* what I do or do *not* want to do, what is or is *not* good for me! And after I'd just got through telling you I wasn't a child!" She glared at him, then looked more closely and felt her anger getting sidetracked.

"You're wet!" she declared, then asked uncertainly, "Were you in the shower?"

"No, I was—"

"Aren't you going to let me come in? I am bare-footed, you know." To her bemusement, her voice seemed to have grown husky. It wasn't as if she hadn't seen his body before, but there was something about the towel, and the way he had it knotted, that made her quite certain there was nothing but Zack underneath it.

Impulsively she reached out and brushed glistening drops of water from one smooth pectoral mound. "And you . . . are getting cold."

"No, I'm not."

"Yes, you are." She brushed the backs of her fingers across a flat nipple and the hard little bump at its center.

He caught her wrist. "Dammit, Maddy. What do you think I am? Do you have any idea how hard it was to say good night to you?"

She gazed steadily at him and said bluntly, "Then why did you?"

"I told you—"

"You told me about holding on to each other . . . comforting each other. I don't see anything wrong with that." It was too soon to tell him how she really felt about him. She didn't have the courage to say the words. Maybe she never would. Which was maybe why she wanted so desperately to *show* him . . .

She took a deep breath, shoring up her crumbling self-confidence. "Zack, I don't want to be alone tonight—not after all we've . . . all that's been said. I don't think you do either."

"Maddy." He took a deep breath and let it out in a sigh. "Are you sure you know what you're doing?"

"Zack. Recent behavior to the contrary, I *am* a grown woman. Give me credit for knowing my own mind. But please." She paused for a small gust of nervous laughter. "If you leave me standing out here on your doorstep much longer, you won't have to say good night, because I'm about to lose my nerve. Zack . . . tell me honestly: Do you want me to go? If you *really* want me to go, I'll leave."

She stared at him, feeling her legs weaken, hearing her heartbeat like thunder in her ears. After several eternities he shook his head and muttered thickly, "No. I don't want you to go."

She lifted her hands, then let them drop, and made a frustrated, whimpering sound. Zack held out his hand. She put hers into it and stepped over the threshold. The door's soft closing seemed symbolic. If she'd gone too far this time, there was no going back.

"Maddy . . ." Her name was a sigh in the darkness. His hand closed on the nape of her neck. "I'm glad you're here."

Tiny electrical currents of anxiety ran around inside her. A hiccup of laughter pushed up through her throat. "Zack, I'm afraid you'll have to tell me . . . I don't know quite where we go from here. I'm not . . . used to this sort of thing."

His hand tightened for an instant on her neck. She heard a soft snort of irony. "What makes you think I am?"

She caught her lower lip between her teeth and stared at his dark outline. "You're not?"

The dry rustle of his laughter stirred the darkness. "Driving for Olympic gold doesn't leave much time for . . . other things. And afterward, I was overwhelmed by all the attention. Carol was the first girl who didn't make me feel like some kind of freak, and we married when I was barely twenty-one. She was two years older. And after she died . . . Look, do you really want to stand here and discuss my sexual track record?"

Maddy heard the vulnerability vibrating through the exasperation in his voice and let her smile come into hers. "No, I don't." She put out her hand and touched the tense muscles of his belly. Beneath the cool, water-chilled skin she could feel vibrant heat and ripples of inner trembling, like the shivers that were turning her own insides to jelly. Tenderness poured through her like warm rain, nourishing her confidence.

Zack's hand turned upward beneath her hair to cradle her head. He brought his mouth to within a hair's breadth of hers, then stopped there, because her palm was still pressing against his stomach, holding him away. She touched his mouth with her smiling lips and slid her hand across the smooth plane of his abdomen to find the knot that held his towel together. When she loosened it he made a sound and a reflexive movement. The towel slid to the floor.

Against her mouth he whispered, "No fair . . ."

Maddy answered, "All's fair . . ."

She caught her breath and held it, standing very still as his free hand slid over her shoulder and down, taking her dress with it. The bodice's stretchy fabric yielded, and Maddy slowly pulled her arm from its sleeve. She felt his cool hand on the heated skin of her rib cage and sucked in air—a tiny, sustaining gasp. Zack's lips touched hers tenderly, reassuringly. His mouth monitored her quick, shallow respirations as his hand followed the neckline of her dress diagonally upward across her body to the other shoulder . . . and then over it. With slow and gentle pressure he pulled the dress down to her waist, eased it over the swell of her hips, and let it fall, with a rustling sigh, to the floor.

Maddy stood in the puddle of discarded clothing, wearing only the plainest of white nylon panties, touching him only with one palm against his belly. Her head still rested in the support of his hand. Her lips barely brushed his, mingling their warm breaths. Electricity crackled between them; heat and a strange aching pressure filled her body; tremors shook her so that she could barely stand. She spoke his name, and was shocked to hear it emerge as a whimper.

In response, he made a low sound—half hunger, half triumph—and finally brought her mouth to his. Keeping space between their bodies, he claimed her mouth, making it seem almost part of his own. Maddy stood as one drugged, with her hands resting forgotten on his waist, oblivious to everything but the rising flood of sensation in her own body. She'd never felt like this . . . never imagined it was possible to feel like this. She was drowning . . . she ached . . . she wanted . . . *something*.

She wanted *Zack*.

She felt his hands slide up over her ribs, brush the sides of her breasts, then gently cover them. His hands were a comforting warmth, soothing the ache *there*, at least. She moaned softly and leaned forward. His fingers sought her nipples, circled them with feathering strokes, then rubbed them with more direct, insistent pressure. A bolt of fire shot through her and settled, throbbing, in the lower part of her body. She gasped and tore her mouth from his, arching her head back and gripping his back for support.

Zack made that sound again, that low, primitive growl of need and dominance, and lowered his mouth to her throat. His hands stroked downward, spanning her ribs, her waist, slipping inside her panties to caress the smooth, taut skin of her belly. She moaned again and pushed against his hands, needing him on a level that was purely instinctive. When one hand moved between her thighs to cup the center of that tormenting pressure, she shuddered and cried out, "Zack—please . . ."

In answer to her plea he jerked her panties over her hips and caught her buttocks in his hands, pressing her hard against him. She gave a little gasp of shock at the unfamiliar shapes and textures of his body, then wrapped her arms around him and strained closer.

As she clung to him, trembling, Zack lifted his head, said thickly, "Time to move, babe," and, in the very best Prince Charming tradition, lifted her into his arms.

Maddy gave a husky gurgle of surprise and pleasure and muttered, "I *knew* there was a third choice!"

Zack uttered a groggy and bewildered, "What?" Maddy whispered, "Nothing . . ." and buried her hot face in the curve of his neck.

Zack was every bit as strong as he'd claimed to be. He carried her easily, effortlessly, making her feel both weak and cherished. And when she felt the cool, crisp texture of the sheets against her back, with

Zack a real and solid presence above her, she discovered that that could be a devastatingly erotic combination. . . .

She was drugged with desire, her body both heavy and tense with wanting. She was filled with pressure, and at the same time empty. She wanted Zack with an urgency that bordered on madness.

"Maddy, sweetheart . . ." His hand brushed her forehead, and she nodded, though she didn't know or care what he wanted to tell her. "Maddy . . . you're not . . . Are you protected?"

She shook her head frantically, almost angrily. "No. But it's all right—*I'm* all right . . . right now." She didn't know whether that was true or not and didn't care. She laced her fingers through his hair and arched her back, silently pleading.

His hand ran down her body, stroking, gentling. She felt the silky caress of damp hair as he lowered his head to her breast, then the rasp of his face on her tender skin. His mouth was a warm, liquid torture.

She shook her head wildly and dug her fingers into his shoulders. She moved her legs and turned her lower body toward him, searching . . . and still he went on caressing her, his hands leaving trails of fire wherever they touched, following her body's curve over back, bottom, and thighs. . . .

It occurred to her that he was trying to take it easy on her account, and she didn't know how to tell him it wasn't what she wanted. *Needed.* The pressure and tension in her were intolerable—she was going to explode. Shaking, she cried, "Zack!—"

He lifted his head and looked down at her, and she whispered, "Please . . ."

His hand slipped under her; her arms circled his neck as he lifted her hard against him. It was instinct that made her shift her legs to make a place for him, and he moved at last into the cradle of her body. His mouth found her throat, and he felt the wild cadence of her pulse as he pressed into her.

She tried to stifle the sharp gasp of shock and pain, but she couldn't. That, and her body's resistance, gave her away. Zack's muscles turned to stone beneath her hands. He lifted his head and said raggedly, "Maddy—dear God—"

"It's all right. Please, Zack."

"Why in the world didn't you tell me?"

"I didn't know how." She felt out of breath and vaguely testy. "It's not the kind of thing you can go around announcing."

"I should have known . . . should have guessed. Maddy, how—"

"Zack." She laughed shakily and felt her stomach bump against his. "Do you want to lie here and discuss my sexual track record *now*?"

He touched his forehead to hers, and she felt him begin to shake with silent laughter. "Ah, Maddy . . ." he said brokenly. "Are you sure?"

"Of course I'm sure. Unless you—?"

He silenced her with his mouth, with a deep and tender kiss. "That answer your question?" he asked thickly when he finally lifted his head. "It's just that this is a new experience for me."

"Well, me too," she said. He began to laugh again.

When their laughter had expired into soft, fitful gusts, Zack cleared his throat and said, "Let's see . . . Where were we?"

"Here." Maddy tipped her chin up and caught his lower lip between her teeth. Her fingers feathered through his hair as she teased his mouth with her tongue.

"Oh, yeah . . ." Once again his hand stroked downward along the side of her body, then slipped under her thigh and drew it gently outward. She stirred, and moved against him.

"Maddy . . ." He looked down at her in the darkness. "Maddy . . . sweetheart, please let me go slowly. Now that I know, there's no reason I should have to hurt you."

She nodded, sighed, and let her hands glide over the smooth skin of his back. "Yes," he murmured approvingly. "Relax. Trust me."

She did trust him. Tension melted. Her body became liquid, molten, pliable. This time he entered her slowly, tenderly, letting her body adjust itself around him. When he began to move, it seemed to her as natural as breathing to move too. The rhythms felt like part of her—like her own heartbeat. *He* was a part of her.

The rhythms didn't change, but somehow that melted-honey warmth inside her became the aching pressure she'd felt before. And again it seemed intolerable. Things were beyond her control. She thought, in one moment of pure panic, that she really would explode. But Zack—Zack was in control, and she trusted him! She surrendered, then, to the fire and strength in his body, and when she did, something inside her gave way, releasing a whole series of sweet explosions. . . .

Zack's hand was stroking her forehead. His lips roved, touching wherever they could—her eyelids, nose, mouth, ears, throat, chin. He held most of his weight away from her, but she could feel his heart knocking crazily against her chest, and the heat of him deep inside her.

She sighed and muttered, "Amazing."

He seemed to understand what she meant. He kissed the tip of her nose and whispered, "I know."

When he left her she made a small noise of protest. He placed his hand on the moist hollow of her stomach, a caress of reassuring intimacy, and whispered, "Just for a second, sweetheart."

She drifted, then, in a state of sensual lethargy that was reminiscent of another kind of floating . . . in warm, churning bubbles. She heard Zack return, and the bed sank beneath his weight. She reached for him, but instead he caught her hand and carried it to his mouth. She felt something warm and soft—a washcloth—gently bathe her body.

"This will make you feel more comfortable," he said softly.

Comfortable? "I am comfortable," she mumbled, finding it a tremendous effort just to move her lips. "I feel . . . wonderful."

His chuckle held both pleasure and relief. His weight shifted; then light altered the texture and density of her eyelids. She gave a sharp cry of protest and covered her eyes with her hand. The light dimmed, but did not go out.

Zack touched her face, then covered her throat with his hand and lightly stroked up and down. "Hey, what's the matter? I just want to look at you." He lifted her hand away from her face and said firmly, "Maddy, open your eyes."

The bedside lamp gave the room a gentle illumination, leaving Zack's eyes in shadow and softening some of the rugged lines of his face. In that twilight his smile was a glow that warmed her like spring sunshine.

"You're not still ashamed of your body, are you?" His hand slid down her throat and chest, rounded delicately over her breasts, and stroked across the relaxed concavity of her stomach to rest on the moist and downy mound below. Where his hand touched her, her skin turned a warm, rosy pink, matching the color in her cheeks. Ashamed? she mused. Well, no . . . probably not. But then, what was this feeling that was turning her, under the heat lamp of his gaze, into one huge all-over blush?

"Do you have any idea," he asked with wonder in his voice, "how beautiful you are?"

"I didn't think you'd noticed," she mumbled, then laughed at herself for sounding like a petulant debutante.

Zack looked tenderly amused. "What do you mean, you didn't think I'd noticed!"

"Well, if you must know, I bought a new dress especially to impress you tonight—although I didn't know at the time it was you I was supposed to impress—and you didn't notice a thing."

He gazed at her for a moment in exasperation, then leaned over to kiss her. "Oh, I noticed," he said, a new huskiness in his voice. "But Maddy, don't you know that what's beautiful about you doesn't have anything at all to do with the way you're dressed? Or," he added thoughtfully, "undressed . . ." He ducked his head to touch his lips to one pink nipple, drew back to look at it, then lowered his head once more, this time to lave the sensitive aureole with his tongue. He drew back once more to examine the results of his ministrations, leaving her glistening with the moisture from his mouth.

The alternating warmth and chill made her shiver and drew both nipples into aching erection. Zack smiled and chuckled with satisfaction as he slowly let his gaze trail upward to meet her eyes.

Something strange was happening to Maddy; she was discovering that she *liked* having him look at her. She loved the way his eyes seemed to touch her like caressing fingers, the way they kindled, like coals coming to life when someone blows softly on them. She moved languidly, sinuously, like a cat stretching, and saw the glow in his eyes become flame.

"Well," she murmured demurely, "I don't know what to say. . . ."

His hand slowly began to draw circles on her belly. "Just say, 'Thank you, Zachary.' "

"Thank you, Zachary. Oh!" She caught her breath as his fingers dipped between her thighs. "By the way, I think . . ."

"Yes?"

"I think . . . you're beautiful too! *Zack*—"

"Well," he said, laughing softly, "now I guess *I* don't know what to say."

"Don't say anything. Just . . ." His hands were tormenting her with feather strokes, making it hard to talk. She caught his hand and held it against her. "Just . . . 'Thank you, Maddy.' "

He captured her other hand and carried it to his body. "Thank you, Maddy."

Her eyes flew open in momentary shock, then drifted down on a smile. "Hello *again*, Zachary," she murmured.

He made love to her slowly this time, showing her with great tenderness and sensitivity all the ways her body could give and receive joy. He left the lights on, so she could see the pleasure she brought to him, and her own, mirrored in his eyes.

When she was limp and somnolent again, and about to drift off to sleep cuddled close in Zack's arms, Maddy realized that she not only knew she was beautiful. For the first time in her life she *felt* beautiful. Never again, with Zack, at least, would she ever feel shy and dismayed by her own body.

She moved her head and touched her lips to his shoulder. "Thank you, Zachary . . ." she murmured, even though she knew he was already asleep.

Maddy woke before Zack did and lay for a while examining the newness of waking up in the morning with a man beside her. Well, not any man, of course, but *Zack*. She decided that was a very important distinction.

The next thing she decided, with some surprise, was that she felt absolutely no guilt. How could something be wrong that gave her such a profound sense of *rightness* and well-being?

The third thing she decided was more in the form of a confirmation: She loved the man beside her, deeply and without reservation.

Though he certainly wasn't a *neat* person, she conceded, gazing at his tousled head with tender amusement. The bed, unmade to begin with, was a twisted tangle of bedclothes, half of which had fallen onto the floor, where they mingled with various discarded items of Zack's wardrobe to form an amorphous pile. Memories of what had caused the bed to be in such a state assailed her, making her feel remarkably smug, like an indolent cat.

It became impossible to lie in bed. She was hungry, and she needed a bathroom. And she'd love a shower, too, but wasn't sure just how "at home" she should make herself in Zack's bathroom. She didn't want to wake him, but at least she could brush her teeth. That brand-new toothbrush she'd found last night after her losing battle with the champagne was down the hall, in the other bathroom.

Easing herself carefully away from Zack's inert form, Maddy crept out of bed and stood up. After a moment's indecision, she bent and sorted through the twisted bedclothes until she had untangled a sheet, which she wrapped around herself like a toga.

Not neat, she thought, but clean. The sheet smelled of fabric softener, and very subtly and evocatively of Zack and of her and the night just past.

Something warm and incandescent spread through her. She looked back once more at the long, tanned body sprawled across the bed, took a deep, tremulous breath, and went out, leaving him in blissful oblivion.

A stop in the bathroom took care of her most pressing needs, but now the clamor in her stomach became impossible to ignore. Hitching her sheet around her, Maddy padded out to the kitchen. As she passed the front entry she saw her shoes, dress, and Zack's towel still lying where they had fallen. Graphically detailed memories made a star-burst inside her as she bent to pick them up and drop them, somewhat pointlessly, into a chair.

Amazing, she thought for the hundredth time. She hadn't known about any of this.

She hadn't known her body could feel like this, tender in places, but awake and tingling in every nerve and cell and pore. She hadn't known before what it meant to say, "My heart is full." She hadn't dreamed it could be so wonderful to love, and be loved—

But wait. Zack hadn't said anything at all about love.

Maddy found herself in the kitchen, staring down at the clutter Zack had left on the counter last night. Her spirits suddenly felt as cold and limp as the stack of untouched toast. Zack had mentioned need and friendship and mutual comfort—even, in a less direct way, desire—but had never, in any way, direct or otherwise, talked about love.

Her stomach growled. She picked up a piece of leathery toast and bit into it, chewing thoughtfully as she examined her feelings. Presently she swallowed and took a deep breath.

Well, okay. She'd faced that reality and decided that she didn't care. She'd concluded long ago that Zack was probably still carrying too much pain around with him to be capable of love anyway. For now, it was enough that he needed her.

Never a very discriminating eater, Maddy polished off that piece of toast and one more, and, in the absence of anything that looked like a coffeepot, a glass of milk. She drank it slowly, sitting at the kitchen table, gazing out at the pool. This, she realized, must have been where Theresa had been sitting when she'd caught Zack kissing her. . . .

It was a beautiful June morning, with the fog already burning away. Beyond the pool deck and the emerald dichondra, flowering shrubs were rampant. Hummingbirds darted about, elusive but captivating flashes of iridescence. The air was a golden shimmer, alive with birdsong.

Sunshine had turned the turquoise rectangle of the pool into a jewel set in terra cotta and jade. Maddy sat staring at that sparkling water for a long time. Then she got up, rinsed her milk glass and set it carefully in the sink, secured her toga, and walked down the stairs to the basement. There she paused to take a deep breath, then pulled open the glass door and stepped with determination into the morning.

Zack went looking for Maddy and found her on the deck. He paused inside the glass door to stare at her as she stood with her back to him, gazing at the pool as if entranced. She looked like a goddess in her sheet toga, with the sun turning the tumbled cascade of her hair to burnished gold. The sheet had slipped low in the back, baring the seductive and graceful curve of her spine. Athena, strolling the gardens of Olympus.

Not entirely certain that the familiarity she'd acquired during the night with his nude body would carry into broad daylight, he stepped back from the door before she could turn and see him. He rummaged in the closet for a reasonably presentable bathing suit and stepped into it. Then he went out to Maddy and dropped a good-morning kiss onto the lush curve of her shoulder.

" 'Mornin', sunshine." He wrapped his arms around her and stood very still, with his head lowered next to hers, just immersing himself in the scent and feel of her.

"Hi." Her voice was shy and breathy, but with an underlying huskiness that he hadn't heard before . . . except, come to think of it, when she'd turned that dragon of hers into a puppet Mae West.

He felt her cheek move as she smiled, and she lifted a hand to touch his hair.

"You were up pretty early, considering," he said.

She laughed low in her throat, a wonderfully sexy sound. Zack had a feeling that everything she said and did from now on was going to have that connotation for him. It might get to be a problem. . . .

"I was hungry," she said.

"Hmm. Find anything to eat?"

More of that delicious laughter. "*Toast.*" He groaned. "No, it wasn't bad—really. I hated to see it all go to waste. And I had some milk. Couldn't find the coffee."

"Coffee's bad for you."

"I knew it," she said with a sigh. "A certified health nut."

"Nobody's perfect," he acknowledged, nuzzling her neck. "Hey, I love your toga. Let's see . . . What was it you did to my towel last night?"

"Zack! Don't you dare. Stop that—" She whirled away from him, clutching her sheet and laughing. "Actually, I was just standing here, thinking . . ."

" 'Bout what?" He folded his arms across his chest in a consciously arrogant, completely masculine stance.

She grinned at him and muttered, "Well, that too. But I was thinking about . . . what we discussed last night. My problem."

"Yeah?" Knowing it was important to her, he made an effort to put a damper on his libido. For the moment. "And?"

"And I was wondering if it had done any good. You said it would help to talk about it, and I did feel better last night, but I don't know if it's changed anything. I can't believe the fear could be gone, just like magic."

"And were you thinking that this might be a good time to try it out?"

She nodded. He went to her and put his hands on her arms. "Sweetheart, I'm game. But don't expect too much of yourself, okay? Talking about your problem is only the beginning. You're right—it isn't magic."

"I want to try." Her gaze was steady, and there was a stubborn look to the set of her mouth. He smiled and kissed her.

"Okay, babe. One problem, though. What are you going to wear?"

He was laughing, but she looked really crestfallen.

She breathed a little "Oh . . ." of chagrin and put her fingers to her lips. "I don't have anything."

"Well," he said judiciously, "you don't really need anything, I suppose."

"Zack! It's broad daylight!"

He lifted his hands. "We're completely private here. No one to see but me."

She chewed her lip in confusion, torn between a lifelong habit of modesty and one of life's primal temptations: the joy of *skinny-dipping*.

"Wait. On second thought," Zack amended hurriedly when he saw a dewy flush of excitement tinge her cheeks, "I think it might be a little too distracting for the teacher. Come on, let's see what we can find."

The best he could come up with was a white T-shirt that came about to mid-thigh on her. A suit bottom stymied him completely. Most of his suggestions so horrified Maddy that she finally pushed him outside in exasperation and announced that she'd take care of the problem herself, thanks!

When she eventually came back out to the pool, pink-cheeked and ruffled and looking like a child in a nightshirt, Zack couldn't resist asking, with the hush of suppressed laughter in his voice, what she was wearing under it.

"My *underpants*," she loftily informed him.

"And what, dare I ask, are you going to do for underpants when . . . um . . . eventually it becomes necessary to . . . ah . . ."

She gave him a quelling glare. He cleared his throat and attempted to arrange his features in an expression of earnestness and responsibility.

"*If* you can get your mind out of my underwear," she said, "we can get down to business—"

It was no use. Zack became convulsed with laughter. Maddy tried her best, but when he hauled her into his arms he felt her body shaking with mirth. "Hush," he said sternly, breaking into fitful chortles, "this is serious stuff."

Which, of course, they both knew it was. Maddy's bathing costume wasn't *that* funny. It was just a safety valve for the tension they were all too aware of, an antidote for the dread that lurked just beyond the silliness.

They managed to keep their faces straight until Maddy hopped off the edge of the pool into the water. Trapped air inflated the T-shirt like a pair of water wings. It rose in a billow around Maddy's chin, baring her midriff and the now totally transparent panties below. Zack gazed at her raptly and murmured, "I think I'm going to enjoy this."

She glared at him and deflated the shirt, submerging herself to her neck to make certain it was thoroughly wet. When she straightened up again, looking smugly triumphant, he shook his head in wonder and said, "I *know* I'm going to enjoy this!" The wet T-shirt was doing what wet T-shirts are famous for doing—defining her magnificent breasts in minute detail, and far more tantalizingly than if they'd been totally bare.

Maddy glanced down at herself and did her best to look disgusted. "Really, Zachary. If you are through behaving like an adolescent voyeur—"

"But when I *was* an adolescent, I didn't have *time* to be a voyeur," Zack protested. "Gimme a break!"

For an answer to his plea Maddy aimed a sizable splash at his face. Zack responded with an outraged bellow. After the ensuing tussle had been brought to a predictable and mutually satisfying conclusion, Zack lifted his mouth from Maddy's and whispered, "Ready?"

Her eyes searched his, and she nodded.

"Okay, babe. We're going down together. I'm going to be touching you, but I won't hold you. You can come up any time you want to. Okay?"

Again her reply was a quick nod. She hadn't taken her gaze from his face. Her lips were parted and still moist from his kiss, and her hands were resting on his shoulders, one loosely hooked around his neck. His arms encircled her, but not tightly. Seconds ticked slowly by, and his heartbeat counted them, one by one. It was like being poised on the platform, awaiting the starter's gun—a moment of frozen eternity.

"Ready . . . set . . . take a breath, hold it . . . *now.*" Zack sent up a prayer for her and slipped under the water, needing all his concentration to keep from tightening his arms around her. He half-expected her to balk, but she didn't. In an agony of suspense he watched her face as she submerged. She kept her eyes and mouth pressed tightly shut, while her hair fanned out around her in golden waves, like every boy's mermaid fantasies.

He'd expected her to stay under for no more than an instant, but again she surprised him. He counted, in growing wonder and elation, to five, to ten . . . and then, as he felt her body tense, he nearly exploded out of the water in order to beat her to it. He wanted—he had—to be there, to see her face.

She erupted from the water in a cascade of silver, like a sea goddess, or a water sprite. Her face was radiant. Drops of water sparkled on her cheeks and lashes like tiny diamonds. She gasped for breath and cried, "I did it, I did it. Zack, *I did it!*"

She hugged him hard, while her body shook with laughter and sobs.

Zack didn't say anything at all. He couldn't. He held her quaking body as tightly as he dared, because he was shaking as badly as she was. As he bowed his head and pressed his wet face against hers, he wasn't at all ashamed that some of the moisture was his own tears. . . .

Zack had stood alone on the topmost step of the victor's platform, with the weight of gold on his chest and the eyes of the world on him, listening to his national anthem and watching his country's flag rise slowly before him, and had felt a similar surge of overwhelming emotion.

But he'd never known a sweeter victory than when he heard Maddy cry with breathless exhilaration, "Zack, I want to do it *again!*"

Ten

Amazing.

That word was becoming the most frequently employed in Maddy's mental vocabulary.

These days everything amazed her. The weather—no June fog! How amazing. Just clear days, hot and beautiful, with blue sky and no smog, perfect for going to the beach. Perfect for lying around Zack's pool. Perfect for swimming lessons.

Flowers amazed her. She'd never noticed so many before. And then there were birds—especially sea gulls, and the little green hummingbirds in Zack's backyard.

Oh, and food! How amazing that cold toast and milk with Zack should taste so good—better than prime rib at an expensive restaurant with anyone else. Just sharing an apple with Zack was more exciting than tasting caviar for the very first time.

But it was people that amazed her the most. There was Dahlia, who never, never smiled, but never judged, either. And Jody, who, since the night of her fire-pit christening party, had been displaying a most extraordinary and unprecedented degree of tact. Larry, who had subjected Maddy to his professionally perceptive scrutiny and declared that she was positively glowing these days, and asked what she was on, some kind of health kick? When Maddy, trying not to blush, told him Zack was teaching her how to swim, he merely remarked blandly, "Well . . . swimming seems to agree with you. Keep it up."

And Theresa was . . . Well, Maddy had decided there was another word to describe that little girl.

She was *irrepressible,* Maddy thought as she gazed at Theresa, perched like a small brown elf on a high stool in front of Maddy's work table.

Theresa was making a puppet out of an old sock, and was busily cutting and gluing scraps of felt and yarn and humming bits and pieces of "Shall We Gather at the River?" A slanting finger of sunshine from one of the skylights touched her head with amber and threw her shadow across Corry, who was sprawled in the middle of everything. The cat was trying to disrupt the project by flicking his tail through the pile of scraps like a feather duster. The tail seemed to have life and personality of its own, and Theresa was playing hide and seek with it and interrupting both her song and her work with giggles.

A bright, happy little girl, Maddy thought, with an outgoing nature and sweet disposition—if you discounted a stubborn streak and a tendency to argue *all* the time. Who would ever guess, watching her now, that barely a month ago she had been a bruised and frightened victim of abuse?

Theresa, Maddy was only too well aware, was one of the lucky ones. She'd been discovered and rescued from a bad situation before any permanent damage had been done. And since then she had been surrounded by nothing but love, thanks to Larry Whitlaw, a warm and very special lady named Dottie Frownfelter, thanks to Dahlia, and Maddy, and of course . . . Zack.

Zack was the most amazing thing of all. He was more than amazing. He was a miracle.

In just a few weeks he'd gone from legend—a gold-medal smile on a billboard or television screen—to awe-inspiring superhero—Aquaman!—to a human being made distant and untouchable by tragedy, and finally, incredibly, to teacher, lover . . . *friend*. Not a superhero at all, but a wonderfully human man, with strengths and weaknesses, virtues and faults. He was quick-tempered and stubborn, gentle and incredibly patient. True, he *was* a health nut, and he wasn't going to win any neatness awards, but he was kind and sensitive and loving.

What amazed Maddy about herself was how she could know someone so well and love everything about him—including his faults—so much, and still manage to keep it all hidden away inside!

It wasn't that she was afraid to have Zack know how she felt about him. Where he was concerned, she didn't really have much false pride. But she had an idea that love like hers would be an awful burden to someone like Zack. Someone who *cared*, but who couldn't love. She told herself that if she were patient and gave him time to heal, someday he might fall in love with her. Until then, she wouldn't burden him with the responsibility for *her* love and her vulnerability.

It was hard, though, to keep her love from showing. Sometimes she felt as if she were walking a tightrope—without a net. One word, one look, a gesture could give her away. The hardest times were those when he let his need for her show. Times when he talked of Josh or Carol. Times when he told her of his hopes for adopting Theresa, and his fears . . .

There was a sharp knock on the door. Theresa and Maddy both called, "Come in!" then laughed with sheer joy, because they knew it could only be Zack.

Maddy realized the instant she saw him that this was going to be one of the tough times. . . .

He walked straight to them with a determined smile on his face, dropping one hand to squeeze Theresa's shoulder as he found the nape of Maddy's neck with the other. Maddy could feel his fingers burrow through her hair like small creatures looking for warmth and comfort. She sensed the tension in him—tension that showed in the set of his jaw, the lines around his mouth and between his eyes, tension that radiated from him like heat.

"Hi, squirt. Whatcha doin'?" He planted a quick but noisy kiss on Theresa's cheek as he leaned forward to see.

"I'm makin' a *snake!*" Theresa proudly announced, and, raising her sock-covered arm, added in a fearsome growl, "An' I'm gonna *eat you up!*"

"Oh, yeah? Well, Mr. Snake, you don't look big enough to me!"

"Well . . . I can eat your nose! *Grum grum grum* . . ." Theresa's "snake" opened its bright pink mouth and engulfed Zack's nose.

"Ouch! Hey, my poor old nose has had enough grief! Gimme a break!"

The roughhouse that ensued routed Corry and swept Theresa and her snake off the stool and, along with most of the puppet materials, onto the floor. Zack wound up flat on his back with Theresa bouncing triumphantly on his stomach, proclaiming, "Got you now! An' I'm gonna chomp your nose off!"

"Ow! Help! Uncle! I give up! Enough already, doggone it! *Maddy!*"

"Don't look at me," Maddy said, laughing as she held up her hands. "You got yourself into that."

"*You* showed her how to make the confounded snake!"

"The snake was all her idea." Maddy shrugged with elaborate innocence. "Don't ask me why, but give a kid a sock and tell him to make a puppet, and he always comes up with a snake. Or maybe a sea serpent. *Maybe* a dinosaur . . ."

"What *I* don't understand—" Zack grunted, then disengaged himself at last and held Theresa at arm's length while he got to his feet "—is why kids are always so cotton-pickin' *carnivorous. Ouch!*" Theresa's snake was busily chomping its way up Zack's leg.

Maddy relented and, sweeping Bosley onto her arm, wrapped the dragon's soft tail loosely around Theresa's neck.

"Hey, honey," she crooned in Bosley's Mae West voice, nudging Theresa's cheek with the dragon's nose. "That's no way to treat a handsome man."

Theresa giggled and squirmed delightedly as the dragon's crest tickled her neck.

"Look, kid," Bosley went on, "you can catch more flies with honey . . . you know what I mean?"

Theresa wrinkled her nose and looked perplexed. "Catch *flies?* Yuck!"

The dragon sighed. "Honey, have you got a lot to learn! Pay attention." Maddy moved the dragon sinuously up Zack's arm, bumped its head under his chin, and fluttered its eyelashes. "Hello, big boy," she crooned. "Why don't you . . . come up and see me sometime?"

Zack blinked and looked dazed, then glanced down at Theresa and rose to the occasion. "Any time you say, shweetheart," he muttered out of the side of his mouth in a passable Bogie impression. He pointed to his cheek. "How's about a little kiss?"

"Oooh, honey," Bosley murmured, and, lowering her lashes, planted a demure kiss on Zack's cheek.

Theresa was delighted. "I want to kiss Zack!" she cried, bouncing up and down. "I mean, my snake wants to. Can I, please? Can I?"

Zack gave Maddy a smug look and bent down so Theresa could reach him. "Put 'er there, shweetheart," he said, pointing to his other cheek.

Theresa tilted her head to one side and pushed her

tongue self-consciously into one cheek as she raised a suddenly shy "snake" to touch Zack's face.

He closed his eyes and sighed. "Now, that's my kind of snake," he said. He caught the puppet around its "neck" and gave it a resounding smack on its pink felt nose.

Theresa grinned up at Maddy, a look of purely feminine conspiracy. Maddy burst out laughing. "Time to clean up the mess," she said as she hung Bosley back on her stand. "Dottie will be here to pick you up any minute. And no arguments," she added firmly as Theresa showed signs of balking. "That's the deal. We make messes, we clean 'em up. Everybody helps."

"Zack too?"

"Of course."

"Hey, I didn't do any of this!"

"Yes, you did," Theresa said. "You knocked everything off on the floor—didn't he, Maddy?"

"Oh, for Pete's sake . . ." Zack grumbled as he squatted down and began gathering scraps of felt. "Hey—" He winked at Theresa and tugged one of her pigtails. "I have a great idea. After we get this all cleaned up, you want to go get a pizza?" He looked up at Maddy and lifted his eyebrows. She opened her mouth, then closed it again, because Theresa was solemnly shaking her head.

"Can't," she declared. "It's Vickie Frownfelter's birthday, and we're having a cake, with *candles*, and ice cream. And you know what? I helped make the cake! She has to have *lots* of candles. She's sixteen! You know what? Next time I have a birthday, I'm going to have seven candles."

"Wow," Zack said. "I'm impressed. When's your birthday?"

"I don't know. I think it's January, but I'm not sure. I can't ever remember. But it's a long, *long* time." Theresa sighed wistfully.

"Tell you what," Zack said. He balanced on his heels to bring himself to Theresa's level. "This Friday is a birthday, did you know that? It's a birthday everybody gets to celebrate. Know what that is?"

Theresa shook her head.

"Fourth of July!"

Her face lit up and she clapped her hands. "Oh, *yeah!* And we get to have sparkles and firecrackers!"

"Right! How'd you like to go have a picnic and watch some fireworks?"

"Oh, boy! With you?"

"With Maddy and me." He swiveled to look up at Maddy, and she saw more in his eyes than a simple question. "How about it, Maddy?" And then, under his breath, "Can you swing it? Please?"

She smiled at Theresa. "I'll ask Dottie." Love had turned all her insides to warm syrup. She didn't dare look at Zack.

"Oh, boy, a picnic!" Theresa was all bounces again. "I've never been on a picnic. Will there be boats?"

"Boats?" Zack looked blank.

"I saw a picture one time. There was a picnic, and kites up in the sky, and a pond with *boats.*"

"Boats." Zack cleared his throat and looked helplessly at Maddy. She shrugged back. "Um . . . well, I'll have to see what I can do."

"You'd do just about anything for that child, wouldn't you?" Maddy murmured.

They had stood together on her doorstep and watched Dottie Frownfelter's station wagon lumber off through the dark tunnel of avocado trees. When they had turned back into the house and closed the door behind them, Zack had reached for her with a fierce and desperate need. But even while her body was responding to him without reservation, something inside her was aching for him, for the pain in him she couldn't heal. . . .

"Yeah." Zack's sigh whispered through her hair.

His arm tightened around her as he tucked her head under his chin.

"Zack, what is it? What's wrong?"

She felt a surprised chuckle vibrate through his chest. "How did you know?"

Oh, when a woman loves her man as much as I do, she just knows.

Maddy closed her eyes and turned her face to his chest, gently nudging. "Come on, tell me."

His deep breath lifted her head. She heard the familiar rasp of his fingers on his scalp as he ran his hand through his hair. "Ah, Maddy . . . I've just spent most of the day going round and round with people down at the county office—adoption-agency people, child-welfare people—you name one person who has anything at all to do with what happens to that kid, and I've talked to him. Or her. Dammit, Maddy, they all tell me the same thing: My chance of adopting Theresa through regular channels is right smack between slim and none!"

"Oh, Zack . . ."

"They say they have at least three couples—*couples*, Maddy—who are as qualified as I am, and have been waiting longer."

"But the fact that she knows you, loves you, surely that will be taken into consideration!"

"Yeah, I thought so. And it might, if she were a little older. But she's so young. They want her to have a mother, a complete set of parents. They feel it's . . . important to her emotional development, particularly at this stage. Well, sure it is, dammit! But so is having someone who really *loves* her!"

"Zack," Maddy said, resting her hand on the side of his face. "You knew you wouldn't have a very good chance with the adoption agency. I told you that. But you can still go talk to Theresa's aunt and uncle and see if they'll agree to a private transfer of custody. I know how you feel about them, her uncle especially. It would be difficult for you, I know, but—"

"Not difficult," Zack said woodenly, and closed his eyes. "Impossible."

"Zachary, that doesn't sound like you. I know how you feel—"

"You don't understand." He stared fiercely at her, then cast his gaze upward toward the skylight over her bed. "That guy wouldn't sign Theresa over to me in a million years. Hell, he'd probably punch my lights out if I showed up at his front door!"

"Oh, surely that's an exaggeration! Even if he knows who—"

"He knows," Zack said, laughing darkly. "Believe me, he knows who nailed him. Remember my fat lip? The one I had the day of the court hearing?"

Maddy gave a small, shocked gasp. "He *hit* you? Theresa's uncle?"

"Why does that surprise you? Maddy, the man *hits* people!"

"All right, then, he's probably gotten it out of his system. He was bound to be upset, especially that day—"

"Uh-uh," Zack said, looking both grim and rueful.

Maddy said with foreboding, "Uh-oh."

He nodded. "I'm not very good at turning the other cheek. I . . . uh, left him sitting in the courthouse fountain."

Maddy clapped her hand over her mouth, stifling a giggle. She knew it wasn't funny. "Oh, Zack," she whispered, and pressed her cheek to his.

"Maddy . . ." Anguish made his voice raw. His arms came around her so tightly, it hurt, and he pulled her over to lie on top of him. "I can't stand the thought of losing her. I can't. . . ."

She held him as tightly as he held her, feeling the tension of grief tumble through him, trying to absorb his pain into her own body, feeling so terribly helpless.

"Zack," she whispered brokenly after a time, "I just wish there were something I could do to help you."

"Maddy . . ." Her name was a sigh. His hands stroked her hair, then her back. "You do help me, just being here." He went very still for a moment, then suddenly took her face between his hands and raised it so he could look into her eyes. His own eyes were very dark, very intense. Maddy's heart began, inexplicably, to pound. "Maddy, there is something you can do. You can marry me."

Zack knew the minute he said it, he'd made a mistake. He felt her body jerk, as if he'd struck her.

Timing, he thought. *I have rotten timing.*

He knew exactly how it had sounded to her, and what she was thinking. He couldn't even try to make it right without making it worse. If he tried to tell her now that he loved her, it would only sound, at best, like an afterthought, or a rationalization. At worst, it would sound like an out-and-out lie.

So he just went on stroking her hair and back, and repeated it. "Marry me, Maddy." This time he added, "I need you." That, at least, he was pretty sure she'd believe.

It seemed crazy to him to lie here like this with her every curve and hollow meshing intimately with his, and realize that he'd never told her he loved her. He wasn't sure why he hadn't told her. He'd known it himself, for an absolute certainty, since that morning when she'd burst from the water like Neptune's daughter, radiant with joy and triumph.

Part of it was pure cowardice. He didn't know for sure how she felt about him, and wasn't quite up to exposing his own fragile ego to the possibility—however remote—of rejection. He knew she cared for him—she'd never have gone to bed with him otherwise—and there was no denying the physical chemistry between them. Even now, with all that he had on his mind, the sweet weight of her body on his was having a predictable effect.

But Maddy was so darned . . . *susceptible!* She was so compassionate, a sucker for anybody or anything in pain. Look at the way she'd had to insulate herself inside those puppets of hers in order to deal with battered kids. Look at the way she'd gone off the deep end for the first one of those kids to slip in under her guard!

Well, he'd slipped in under her guard, too, using her own fear and vulnerability, and even her compassion, against her. And now he didn't know whether she loved him, or whether she was only responding to his need for her.

It hadn't bothered him, until now. Until now, he'd told himself that, either way, it was enough.

Right now, that thought made him feel bleak and lonely.

She stirred against him. "Do you think it would help?" she asked. Her voice sounded muffled.

The tension inside him bubbled up and escaped in a short, harsh laugh. "Couldn't hurt!"

"What happens," she said slowly, obviously choosing her words carefully, "if they still won't let you have her?"

For a moment his mind went blank, and he thought, *Let me have whom?* All his concentration right now was focused on Maddy. With or without Theresa, he knew he wanted her.

"We'll cross that bridge when we come to it," he said.

Of course, he mused, she would think that if he lost Theresa, he'd need *her* more than ever. *Maddy*, he said silently, *I love you too much. Don't say yes for the wrong reasons!*

Again she stirred in his arms, and lifted her head to look down at him. Her mouth seemed very soft. He saw it quiver slightly before it formed a smile.

"All right, Zachary," she whispered. "I'll marry you."

He stared at her for a long time, his hands framing

her face. She moved slightly—a subtle insinuation that sent responses jolting through him. *Forgive me*, he thought, and brought her mouth down to his.

"You're *what*?" Jody screamed at Maddy over the telephone, causing Maddy to wince and pull the receiver away from her ear. "You're getting—I don't believe it! To whom? Or whom to? Zack. It has to be. I knew it, I just knew there was something going on between the two of you when I saw the way you looked at each other at the party! And here I thought I was planning this big, wonderful surprise! I'll never forgive you for that, Amanda. I felt like such a fool. Hey—congratulations!"

"Thank you," Maddy said, gazing blankly at Bosley's nose. She had picked up the puppet when she sat down to dial the telephone—an automatic reflex.

There was a pause. "Thank you?" Jody repeated. "*Thank you? Is that all you have to say? You call me to tell me you're getting married—out of the clear blue, mind you—to San Ramon's—maybe the world's—most eligible hunk, and then you sit there and murmur demurely, 'Thank you'? Come on, Maddy. Let's have a few details. Just basics. Like *when*, for starters."

"We haven't set an exact date," Maddy murmured, frowning at Bosley. "But soon."

"Soon. You do realize, I hope, that when this gets out it's going to be a media event?"

"With any luck, and a little discretion on the part of certain *friends*," Maddy said warningly, "it won't get out. It's going to be a very small affair."

"How small? San Ramon United Methodist, as opposed to Saint Patrick's Cathedral?"

"Justice of the peace," Maddy said, bracing for the explosion. "Two witnesses. That's why I'm calling. I'd like you to be mine."

There was an ominous silence on the other end of the line. And then an uncharacteristically quiet, "Maddy? What's wrong?"

"Nothing's wrong." Maddy stuck her tongue out at Bosley and dumped the stupid puppet onto its pink felt head. "We just . . . don't want a big fuss, that's all."

"Amanda, I may be loud, but I'm not deaf. I can hear your voice perfectly, and you don't sound happy to me. Certainly not like somebody who's about to marry the man of her—and anyone else's—dreams. Now, what's the matter? Oh, my God, are you pregnant? Are you trying to tell me you guys *have* to get married? Oh, for heaven's sake, it couldn't be. Nobody does that anymore, do they?"

Maddy was laughing, but the laughter hurt her chest. *Well, actually, Jody, yes, we do have to get married. The baby just happens to be six years old.*

"No, Jody, it's nothing like that. It's just . . . well, you know Zack's background. We don't want the media to get hold of it and drag up all the tragedy. You understand, don't you?"

"Sure," Jody said. "I understand. And I understand that there's something here you're not telling me."

"Jody . . ." Maddy sighed. She could hear the hurt in Jody's voice. But though Jody was her best friend and she loved her dearly, there were some things it just took too much effort to explain.

"Oops, there's the door," she said, never more relieved in her life to hear a knock. "Gotta go. Talk to you later—"

"Don't think for a minute you've heard the last of th—"

Maddy gently cradled the receiver and started for the door, tripping over Corry, who was dashing for his position, stage left.

"Uh-oh," Maddy muttered. "A newcomer. Now, I wonder who in the world . . .?"

For a few seconds she couldn't place the nondescript but vaguely familiar-looking woman standing on her doorstep.

"Miss Gordon?" the woman asked hesitantly, clutching her purse as if it were a shield. "I hope I'm not disturbing you. It's . . . I'm Theresa's aunt."

"Oh!" Recognition dawned. "Mrs. Soto! I'm sorry, I didn't—Won't you come in?"

"Oh, please, just call me Carleen." Theresa's aunt smiled nervously and made a self-deprecating gesture with her hand. "Mrs. Soto sounds so . . ." She was looking around her, but Maddy didn't think she was really seeing anything. Even Corry's act was wasted on her—to his disgust.

"Um . . . listen," Carleen said, "I hope you don't mind my coming here like this. I asked at that clinic—Dr. Whitlaw—he told me where I could find you. I thought maybe you wouldn't want to talk to me because of . . . what happened to Theresa, but Dr. Whitlaw said . . ."

"Please," Maddy said. "Won't you sit down?"

Theresa's aunt settled uneasily onto the edge of the couch and placed her purse across her lap, clutching it with one hand while she pushed limp hair away from her face with the other.

"Thank you," she said softly, looking up at Maddy with wide, perpetually worried eyes. "I . . . um . . . I'm really sorry about what happened. You've got to believe that. I really love—" She swallowed, pressed her lips together, and went on. "She was my sister's little girl. After my sister died, I really wanted to take care of her—for Elaine's sake, you know? I really do care about Theresa."

Maddy nodded. "I'm sure you do."

Carleen took a deep breath. "It was okay when she was real little, but then . . . Well, Joe got this new job, and there's a lot of pressure on him, and he's always afraid he's going to get fired. And then when he gets scared, sometimes he drinks too much. And Theresa, she *talks* a lot, and then she argues, and sometimes she doesn't mind, and—"

"I know," Maddy said. "I understand."

Carleen touched her nose with the back of her hand and looked beseechingly at Maddy. "Joe's not a bad guy—he really isn't. But he never did get on with Theresa, and it's probably just as well—Anyway, that's what I wanted to talk to you about."

"What's that?" Maddy encouraged gently, trying to be patient.

"Dr. Whitlaw says once Theresa's made a ward of the county, she'll be put up for adoption."

"That's right."

"He says there's already several people that want her real bad. Is that true?"

"Yes," Maddy whispered. "It's true."

"Yeah, well, I'm really glad about that. All I want's for Theresa to be happy. She's a good kid."

Maddy wordlessly handed Carleen a tissue and waited while she blew her nose. The lump in her own throat was in imminent danger of causing her to explode into tears.

"Anyway," Carleen continued after a moment, giving Maddy a look of apology, "I've been to see Theresa a couple of times—over at that foster home they've got her in—and all she does is talk about somebody named *Zack*. And you. It's always Zack this, and Maddy that. Well, I know Zack is that swimming teacher—the one who reported Joe—because at the hearing, afterward, Joe kind of lost his temper and . . ."

"I know," Maddy said, and cleared her throat. "Zack told me about it." She kept wondering when Carleen was going to get to the point. She didn't want to appear impatient—she knew how hard it must have been for the woman even to come there—but she still had a lot to do to get ready for tomorrow's picnic. She and Zack had gotten permission to take Theresa to the county's fireworks show at Dolores Springs Park, which had a small lake, with canoes and paddle boats. It was important to Zack that this be a special day for Theresa. The hearing was scheduled for Monday morning. This could be the last outing with Theresa they would ever have. . . .

"I was wondering—" Carleen took a big breath. "Do you think this Zack would want to adopt Theresa?"

Maddy stared at Carleen. "Yes. As a matter of fact, he wants very much to adopt Theresa. But you see, there's a problem. He's not married, and even though he's about to be, he's still way down on the list. The county adoption agency has several couples ahead of him."

Carleen was nodding. "I know, I know. That's what Dr. Whitlaw said. But he said people can make private arrangements. That they can agree ahead of time about custody. So . . . couldn't you and Zack—"

"Oh, sure, we'd love to," Maddy said, jumping up from her perch on the arm of the couch. Her voice was sharp, and Carleen was staring at her, but she couldn't help it. "I'm sure your husband can hardly wait to do a favor for the guy who punched him in the stomach and left him sitting in the middle of a public fountain!"

Carleen put her hand over her mouth in a vain attempt to stifle a nervous giggle. Maddy stared at her in exasperation. "Carleen, can I ask you a question? Why did you come to see me about this? Why didn't you talk to Zack? He's the one–"

"Oh, gee, are you kidding?" Carleen gave another nervous titter and clutched her purse. "Joe would kill me if he ever found out I'd talked to *him*. I don't think he'll ever forgive him for that—although he had it coming. Joe hit him first."

"Carleen," Maddy said gently, praying for patience and wishing the woman would just leave, so she could have a good cry and get her frustration out of her system. "If your husband won't even talk to Zack, what in the world makes you think he'd ever agree to give him custody of Theresa?"

Carleen's eyes got very round. She took a deep breath, squared her shoulders, and visibly seemed to pull herself together.

"But that's the thing, see," she said, looking determined. A little scared, but determined. "Zack doesn't need Joe's permission. See, my sister, she never cared much for Joe. In her will, she gave custody of Theresa to *me*. That's all. Just me. I'm Theresa's legal guardian."

Maddy stared at her. She felt strange. Frozen.

Carleen cleared her throat and looked down at her hands. Maddy heard the snap on Carleen's purse click loudly. She watched Carleen's hands dive into the handbag and reappear holding some legal-looking papers. When she gazed back up at Maddy her eyes held a rather touching spark of defiance. There was a pink flush across her cheeks.

"I want—I'd really like for you guys to adopt Theresa. You and Zack. So . . . I went and got the papers." She thrust them at Maddy. "Here they are. If you want to . . . all you have to do is sign them."

Eleven

Dolores Springs Park was several miles from San Ramon, in the coastal foothills. The springs fed a creek, which ran down a canyon crammed with native California sycamores and live oaks, into what had to be a rarity in Southern California—a small, natural lake. The Parks Department had installed boat docks and restrooms and picnic tables, and, at the lower end of the canyon, parking lots and a softball diamond, but otherwise had left things pretty much in their natural state.

The tires of Maddy's car—Zack's Mercedes wouldn't accommodate three—crunched over a layer of live-oak mulch as she pulled into a shady spot and parked.

Theresa was already bouncing out of her seat belt, shouting, "Oh, boy. Where's the lake? I don't see any lake!"

Zack laughed. "Patience, imp. Would I lie? Here, you get to carry the blanket."

"I want to carry the picnic basket!"

"Sorry, squirt. You're just a little bit too small for that. But here, how about this?"

He reached into the back seat and took out the mysterious oblong package he'd been gloating about all morning with maddening secrecy. Theresa scowled at the bundle and turned it over in her hands with open suspicion. "What's *this*?"

"A surprise," Zack said firmly. "Come on. Let's get this safari on the road!"

Maddy locked her car and followed Zack and Theresa up the path, crunching oak debris underfoot. Though loaded down with blankets, a basket, and extra jackets, Zack's step was jaunty. Maddy knew he was determined to make this a happy day for Theresa, even if his own heart was filled with the knowledge that it might be the last day they'd ever spend with her.

When shall I tell him?

Life, Maddy reflected, was full of weird twists and turns. It seemed cruel to keep from Zack one moment longer than she absolutely had to the wonderful news that Theresa was all but his. So why was she still hugging it to herself, like a miser jealously guarding his pot of gold? The custody papers were sitting right there in her purse, the purse she'd left safely locked in the trunk of her car.

Why was it so hard to tell him?

Because she knew perfectly well why Zack had asked her to marry him. He'd hoped a wife would help to swing the adoption board in his favor. If he were assured of gaining custody of Theresa without a wife, would he still want to marry her? Zack was a decent, compassionate man. He would never be so cruel as to withdraw his proposal just because the situation had changed.

But the situation *had* changed. And Maddy knew that, regardless of Zack's principles, she couldn't go through life married to someone who didn't love her.

Any way you sliced it, it was going to be a difficult and painful thing to resolve.

It had been enough that Zack needed her. Now even that would be gone.

"Hurry *up*, Maddy!" Theresa called. She and Zack were waiting for her to catch up. Theresa held out her hand, dancing with impatience. "Give me your hand!"

With Zack and Maddy each holding one of her hands, Theresa took two running steps and lifted both feet off the ground, swinging suspended between the two grown-ups.

Maddy laughed. "Don't you think you're a bit too big to do that?"

"Aw, gee," Theresa grumbled. "How come I'm always either too small or too big!"

"The universal lament of the child," Zack said dryly. "That's the breaks, squirt."

They were ahead of the bulk of the holiday crowd, which would come in later for the fireworks show, on shuttle buses from town. Even so, picnickers had already claimed the available tables, so they staked out a nice spot under a sycamore tree on the gently sloping banks of the lake. It was directly opposite the softball field, where the pyrotechnics experts were busy setting up for the big display later that evening. They would have a good view without being close enough to sustain permanent hearing damage.

Theresa was a little disappointed with the lake at first. The boats were only ugly old canoes, not pretty white sailboats like the ones in her picture. But when Zack told her that the boats in her picture were just toys and that you could actually take a *ride* in these ugly old canoes, she brightened right up, and of course wanted to go in a boat *immediately*.

So all three of them donned bright orange life jackets and spent the early part of the afternoon paddling ineptly around the lake, dodging other canoes and paddle boats, and drenching each other with water from their paddles.

When they had collapsed back on their blanket, laughing and half soaked, Zack reached for his mystery bundle and drew it forth with a flourish.

"Oh, boy," Theresa cried, bouncing up and down on her heels. "Now we get to see the surprise! What is it? Can I see? Hurry up, Zack!"

"Ah-ah. Cool it, squirt. All in good time." Zack was shamelessly milking his moment.

Maddy watched them bend together over the package and felt a surge of love wash through her like a tidal crest. She was glad, at that moment, that neither of them happened to be watching her face. She lowered her head until the spasm had passed, then wiped her cheeks quickly and openly with her hands. Her face was spattered with water, anyway, from the canoe's paddles.

They were having such a wonderful time, she thought, even without knowing that everything was going to be all right. She didn't need to tell him yet. She would wait a little longer. She could be a part of them for just a little longer. . . .

"It's a *kite!*" Theresa shrieked. "A kite, just like in the picture! Can we make it fly, Zack? Can we?"

"That's the idea," he muttered, looking perplexed as he tried to decipher the assembly instructions. He cast Maddy a look of appeal.

She sighed and gazed skyward, then reached for the jumbled pieces. "Piece o' cake," she said smugly a few minutes later as she handed back the assembled kite.

"Hmm," Zack said with grudging admiration. "How'd you do that?"

"Maddy knows how to make things," Theresa explained. "She makes puppets all the time, don't you know that?"

"Handy person to have around," he said softly, smiling into Maddy's eyes. It was the first time all day he'd allowed himself to meet her eyes, and in that moment she saw the fear he'd been trying so hard to hide. And something else too. Something elusive, like a familiar face glimpsed in a crowd. She caught her breath and tried to hold on to whatever it was she'd seen, but it was gone too quickly, hidden behind that smoky veil.

He leaned over to give her a thank-you kiss. Then he and Theresa were dashing off to find an open space in which to launch their kite.

Maddy took a deep breath and opened the picnic hamper. It was their day, Zack and Theresa's. She was the outsider. They didn't *really* need her at all.

They came trooping dejectedly back to the blanket about half an hour later—minus the kite.

"A tree ate it," Theresa said sadly.

"A kite-eating tree." Zack looked thoroughly disgusted. "There really is such a thing, can you believe it? Never mind, squirt," he said, ruffling Theresa's hair. "Next time we'll go to a park with wide-open spaces!"

Next time. He threw Maddy a look that tore at her heart. She almost, *almost*, blurted out the truth to him then and there. But Theresa began exclaiming over the array of picnic goodies Maddy had laid out, and the moment passed.

They ate fried chicken and potato chips, and carrot and celery sticks and black olives, and fresh strawberries as big as small apples and so sweet, they needed no sugar at all. Maddy had bought them at the roadside stand just down the street from her place. There was a bag of peanut-butter cookies, too, from Dottie Frownfelter.

"Because I made 'em," Theresa announced, then conscientiously amended, "Well, I helped."

"Let me guess," Zack said. "You *smashed* 'em, right?"

"Right," Theresa said, giggling.

After they'd finished eating, Theresa wanted to go out in the canoes again.

"Not now," Zack murmured, yawning as he settled himself with his back against the sycamore tree. "Don't you know you're supposed to take a nap after a Fourth of July picnic?"

"Come *on*, Zack." Theresa tugged at his hand, then gave up, recognizing a lost cause when she saw one. "Can I go by myself, then? I'm big enough."

Zack opened one eye and gave her a stern glare. "No, you're not. Don't you go near those boats without me, understand? Hey," he added persuasively as Theresa's chin developed a stubborn tilt. "You know, those fireworks are going to keep us up *way* past our bedtime. Come here and help me catch some z's."

"I'm not sleepy," Theresa said, but curled up next to Zack anyway, and in a remarkably short time was out like a light. . . .

"Hey, sweetheart. Wake up." Zack's words made soft, moist puffs against Maddy's temple. His fingers were stroking her throat. She opened her eyes and found his face inverted an inch or so above hers. "Sorry to disturb you, babe. I need your keys."

"What . . .?"

"Shh. Theresa's still asleep. Car keys. I thought I'd take a bunch of this picnic stuff back to the car right now, so we don't have so much to carry later."

"Oh. Okay." She fumbled in her pocket for the keys to her car. "Zack . . . bring back my purse, okay? I left it in the trunk."

"Sure." He gave her a lingering, upside-down kiss, and whispered, "Sweet dreams . . ."

Maddy woke suddenly, with that sweaty, shaky, adrenaline surge that accompanies an already-forgotten nightmare. She sat up trembling and disoriented, staring around her, terrified without knowing why.

Then suddenly, with shattering clarity, she *knew* why.

She was alone. The blanket was empty. Theresa was gone.

The nightmare terror ebbed slowly with the return of full consciousness, leaving her concerned and mildly annoyed, but not really worried. Theresa couldn't have gone far—wouldn't have gone far. She'd just gone off, in her independent little way, to do some exploring on her own.

"Can I go by myself? I'm big enough."

No. She wouldn't try to take out one of the boats by herself. Zack had expressly told her to stay away from them.

Maddy stood up and walked a little way down the slope toward the docks, shading her eyes against the glare of the setting sun. Could Theresa get past the men who managed the canoe rentals? Probably she could. *But she wouldn't disobey Zack . . . would she?* Then Maddy remembered Carleen saying, "Sometimes she doesn't mind. . . ." And she remembered that stubborn little chin. . . .

She looked around for Zack, then recalled that he'd gone to the car. How long ago had that been? She had no idea how much time had passed, how long she'd been dozing. Long enough, certainly, for a little girl to wake up and completely vanish from her sight.

Maddy began to call, "Theresa? Theresa!" as she walked down toward the lake.

There were several canoes still out on the water, dark silhouettes on a surface of rippled bronze, but she couldn't see against that glare. She called again, cupping her hands around her mouth to make a megaphone, sending her voice across the water.

A thin, childish voice answered. One tiny figure lifted an arm to wave, then stood up. "Hi, Maddy. Look at me! Look what I can do!"

"Theresa! Oh . . . God." Maddy clapped both hands over her mouth and looked frantically around her. Several people were glancing her way, apparently wondering what was happening. "Theresa, honey, stay there! Sit down! Do you hear me? *Sit down!*"

Some of Maddy's urgency seemed to reach the little girl. Suddenly she appeared confused. As she wavered uncertainly between standing and sitting, her paddle slipped from her grasp and fell into the water. She reached for it—an automatic reflex—and then, frightened by the canoe's wobble, tried to regain her balance. It was too late. As Maddy watched in stony horror, Theresa toppled into the gilded water.

She made a pathetically insignificant splash. Maddy's anguished cry covered it completely. Maddy remained frozen, nailed to the end of the dock, until she saw a dark head bob to the surface. Then she closed her eyes tightly, held her nose, and jumped.

As she hit the water she had only one thought: *Not again. Zack can't lose another child like this. Dear God, not again . . .*

Zack was coming down the slope through the sycamore trees when he heard Maddy's scream. It took him a fraction of forever to locate her, poised there on the end of the dock, and another eternity before he'd identified the reason for her cry. When he saw Maddy jump, he whispered, *"No . . . !"* Maddy's purse slipped from his hand as he began to run.

He flew down the hill and thundered onto the dock, scattering the gathering crowd like so many pigeons.

Theresa was treading water, bless her heart, just the way he'd taught her. Zack shouted at her, "That's it, baby, you're doing fine. Just hang in there. I'm coming!"

Hang in there, baby. Please.

Maddy was floundering through the water with a

kind of frantic resolve that had already carried her far beyond her limits. Zack swore with the kind of virtuosity that only comes with sheer emotional overload. The *idiot!* The crazy idiot. She'd learned a lot in three weeks, but there was no way in the world she'd ever make it out as far as that canoe, much less back again with Theresa! What did she think she was going to do? They'd both drown!

They'd both drown.

"Call the paramedics!" he bellowed at the nearest bystander, and launched himself into the water like a human torpedo.

He'd never pushed himself so hard in his life. He wasn't swimming for gold or records now—he was swimming for two people's lives. The lives of the two people he loved most in the world.

As he churned through the water, Zack was torn between the need to keep those two heads in his sight, and the knowledge that he'd gain speed by keeping his head down. He tried to locate them whenever he took a breath, but it was so hard to see.

Theresa's eyes were his beacon, his lighthouse. *Hang on, baby, he pleaded silently. I'm coming. Don't let go. Don't give up. . . .*"

He'd lost sight of Maddy. He couldn't see her anymore.

He reached Theresa, and she clung to his neck. Her thin little body was shaking with cold and fear.

"Easy, sweetheart," he said. "Take it easy. I've got you."

Her voice was a frightened whimper. "Maddy's drownding."

"No! No . . . she's not gonna drown. You hang on here, okay?" Two powerful strokes carried him to the drifting canoe. He hoisted Theresa into it, sent up a fervent prayer, and dove.

The water was murky; he couldn't see a thing. All he could think was, *Dear God, she must be terrified.*

It had to be sheer luck that he found her. He felt

something brush his leg, and, reaching for it, managed to grab a handful of Maddy's hair.

She came up coughing, choking, retching—making terrible, wonderful noises that told him she'd be all right. Theresa, when she saw Maddy, began to howl at the top of her lungs—and that was a wonderful noise too.

Dimly Zack heard the wail of a siren. Other boats were arriving. Strong hands reached down to pull Maddy from his arms. And then all three of them—Zack, Maddy, Theresa—were huddled in the Parks Department rowboat, wrapped in blankets.

No one spoke. Theresa wailed, Maddy coughed, and Zack sat in stony shock as they were rowed back to the shore.

As Zack stepped onto the dock, someone put Theresa into his arms. He held her silently while she wrapped her arms around his neck and hid her face from the crowd. A voice spoke with quiet authority.

"All right, folks. Let's move on back out of the way now. Let us get through here." The fire department's two paramedics helped Maddy onto the deck, then knelt down beside her.

Above the folds of her blanket Maddy's eyes went wide with dismay. "Oh, no," she managed to rasp out. "Zack—you didn't . . . call the *paramedics*?"

It was suddenly too much. Like magma building below the surface of the earth that finally erupts in volcanic cataclysm, Zack's emotions reached the breaking point. He set Theresa down—not gently—and exploded.

"What the hell did you expect me to do? You bet I called the paramedics! Of all the stupid, asinine stunts—What the hell were you trying to do? You can't swim well enough to keep *yourself* from drowning! Hell, Theresa swims better than you do!"

Maddy stared at him while the paramedics went about checking her vital signs with calm efficiency. Zack thought *his* vital signs were probably in worse shape than hers were right now. He took two steps away from her, then whirled back. "What are you trying to do—kill me?"

"Kill you?" she whispered.

He covered his face with one hand, then threw both arms wide. "Yeah! Kill me. Do you think I could survive losing the two people I love most in the whole damn world . . . *twice?*"

One of the paramedics gave him a compassionate glance and held an oxygen mask to Maddy's face. She pushed it away.

"Zack—" Her voice collapsed into a wheezing cough. "Stop it. Look at Theresa. You're scaring her!"

Zack glanced at Theresa, who was shaking violently in spite of the gray wool blanket that shrouded her to her wide black eyes. He looked back at Maddy and snapped, "Yeah, well, that's just *tough.*" He reached out and, ignoring Theresa's flinch, pulled the girl close against his side. "She'll just have to get used to the idea that people who love each other sometimes get *mad at each other. And when they get mad, sometimes they yell. But that doesn't mean they hit!*" He squatted down suddenly and pulled Theresa around to face him. "You hear me, squirt?"

She gave him a slow, awestruck nod.

"Well, let me tell you something else, young lady." He rested his hands on Theresa's shoulders and looked sternly into her eyes. "If you *ever* disobey me like that again, I'm gonna smack your bottom! Got that?"

Another nod. Zack felt himself deflating as the rage and adrenaline that had kept him going slowly ebbed from his system. He heaved an enormous sigh and suddenly hauled Theresa into a great bear hug. He just knelt there, dripping water, holding her while great shudders racked his body. After a few minutes he became aware of a small hand patting his back.

"It's okay, Zack," Theresa was saying. "It's okay. I'm sorry. Please don't be mad."

He took another deep breath. "I'm not mad," he mumbled. "Just scared." He opened his eyes and looked over Theresa's head, searching for Maddy, who, it suddenly occurred to him, had become very quiet.

The paramedic had finally succeeded in getting the oxygen mask over her nose and mouth. Over it, her eyes stared blankly at him. She seemed to be in some kind of shock.

"Is she all right?" Zack asked hoarsely.

"Oh, yeah. She's going to be just fine." The paramedic was already packing up his equipment. "I'd have her checked out by a doctor, though, just to be sure." He called to his partner, who was on his way back to the truck. "Hey, Mike. See if you can intercept that ambulance, will you? We won't be needing it."

Zack stood up, feeling as if his joints had rusted. He offered the paramedic his hand. "Thanks . . ." He couldn't think of what else to say.

The paramedic grinned. "Hey, no sweat. Just glad to have one of these holiday drowning calls turn out all right, for a change." He waved and followed his partner up the hill.

Zack turned to Maddy, who was still sitting huddled in her blanket, staring up at him as if he'd suddenly sprouted an extra head. He squatted on his heels beside her.

"Maddy? Hey, babe, are you all right? I'm sorry I yelled at you—"

She gave her head a quick, violent shake. "No . . . it's okay. I understand." Her voice sounded thick.

He touched her face, drawing his fingers down her cheek. "Then what is it? What's wrong?"

"Zack," she said faintly, "did you say . . . I heard you say . . ."

"Yes? What?" Suddenly his heart was pounding in a way it never did after a race. He began to wonder if something was wrong with him—if maybe he was getting old.

"I heard you say two people . . . Did you mean . . . that you love *me?*"

He could only stare at her, overwhelmed. "Are you *crazy?*" he muttered brokenly.

She slowly nodded, still gazing into his eyes as if transfixed by something she saw there.

"Of course I love you!" His emotions were erupting again, in a way some might have considered unmasculine. He snatched his hand away from her face and gestured wildly with it, so overcome by his need to touch her, to crush her in his arms, that he didn't trust himself to do so without hurting her. "When I think . . . about losing you—When I thought about you down there in that water, sinking . . . When I thought of you dying in that water, when you—"

"Zack!" Her eyes were suddenly round and full of light. Her hands were on his arms, holding him tightly, shaking him. "Zack, I wasn't afraid! I just realized that. I wasn't—not in the same way! I was scared, yeah, but the way anyone would be. It wasn't . . . *terror*, like my nightmares! Zack, I'm okay, I'm really *okay!*"

"Yeah . . ." He took a deep breath, dashed moisture from his cheeks, and shook his head, smiling at her through a blur. "You sure are. More than okay."

"*Zack.*" She was shaking him again. "I've got to tell you something, something wonderful—"

"Lord, I hope so. You'd better be telling me you love me, too, or I'm liable to be taking a walk off the end of this pier!"

"Oh, that too. Of course I lo—"

"What do you mean, '*that too*'!" he said with a growl, just before he lost his grip on his self-restraint and dragged her into his arms.

"No . . ." She was shaking her head frantically, bracing her hands against his chest, and smiling. *Laughing.* Crying.

"I love you, Zachary, and I have wonderful news for you. You won't believe it. Just wait until I tell you!"

When, a few moments later, Zack let go with a whoop of pure joy, there was no one to cast him more than a glance of mild curiosity. The crowd had dispersed, gone back to Frisbees and sparklers and picnic baskets. If anyone thought it the least bit odd that he suddenly gathered the two people he loved most in the world into his arms and hugged them, laughing and crying at the same time, he couldn't have cared less.

Theresa," Zack said some time later. "Maddy and I'd like to ask you something."

They'd decided, in spite of everything, to stay for the fireworks. They'd promised Theresa fireworks; they'd never hear the end of it if they didn't stay. So they sat sandwiched together for warmth, waiting in suspense for the first skyrockets to burst across the darkening sky. Theresa was between Maddy's knees, Maddy between Zack's, with his arms around them both and the blankets wrapped around all three of them. Maddy's purse and its precious contents lay on the blanket beside Maddy's feet.

Theresa tilted her head and said agreeably, "Okay."

"How would you like it," Zack said slowly, pausing every couple of syllables to touch his lips to Maddy's ear, a process that was causing waves of warm shivers to cascade down her spine, "if you could come and live with Maddy and me?"

Theresa was silent for a minute, considering. "That would be good." She swiveled her head to look up at Maddy. "You mean like, you'd be my foster parents 'stead of Dottie?"

"No," Zack said. "I mean we'd be like your real mom and dad. You'd live with us . . . forever."

"Oh." Theresa's head swiveled back. She looked out at the empty sky and shrugged. "I don't think I can." Her voice sounded sad.

Zack looked at Maddy, Maddy looked at Zack, and

they both shrugged. Zack cleared his throat and asked carefully, "Why not?"

"Well, 'cause I have a real mom and dad already. They're in heaven. So nobody can't be my real parents."

Maddy held her breath. She felt a tremor ripple through Zack's chest, but couldn't tell whether it was laughter or something else.

"Well," Zack said, and rested his chin on the top of Maddy's head. After a moment he cleared his throat and went on. "I have a real son, did you know that? His name is Josh, and he's in heaven too. Now, if Maddy and I adopt you, you'll be our real daughter. That's what the law says. So if we can have another real kid, it seems to me you could have another set of real parents."

Maddy felt the pressure of Zack's lips on the top of her head and tilted sideways to press against his shoulder. They both waited tensely while Theresa turned the logic of that over in her mind. After what seemed like forever, they felt her head move up and down.

"Okay. Then it's prob'ly all right."

"Well, okay, then. It's settled." Zack lowered his mouth to the curve of Maddy's neck. She felt his slowly expelled breath like a warm caress. Both the big, solid body against her back and the small, thin one in her arms seemed very still and subdued.

After a while Theresa tipped her head back and asked, "Where would we live? Maddy gots a house, and so do you. I like Maddy's house—you can open up the ceiling and see the sky—but she doesn't have a swimming pool, and I don't think she has enough beds for everybody to sleep in."

"Hmm," Zack said. His voice sounded suspiciously quivery. "That is a problem. How's this? Maddy can keep her house for a special place to make puppets, and you can all come and sleep at my house." He touched his lips to Maddy's ear and whispered, "Okay?"

"Okay," she whispered back, her voice breaking up into laughter.

"That would be good," Theresa decided. "Will I get any brothers and sisters? Real ones, not foster ones, like Vickie Frownfelter."

"Oh," Zack murmured, sending silky shivers down Maddy's neck with his breath, "I think we could probably manage one or two. . . ." She turned to look at him. "Or more. You never can tell." He shrugged placidly as he settled Maddy firmly against him and prepared to field Theresa's next question. It came after another thoughtful silence.

"Will I get a gramma and grampa? Real ones? I've never had a gramma and grampa before."

Zack nudged Maddy, who nodded and held up two fingers. "Yep," he said. "Complete set—two of each."

"Only two?" Theresa's head tilted upward. "What about Dahlia? Can't she be my gramma too?"

"You can ask her," Zack said. "Wouldn't be a bit surprised."

"Okay," Theresa said with a satisfied sigh. "You know what? I think it's gonna be *all right!*"

"Me too," Zack said, and ruffled her hair. Then he wrapped his arms across Maddy's chest and whispered, "How about you?"

"Well," Maddy said, "I do have one question. I hate to ask—it seems so crass—but I just keep wondering . . ."

"What?" he mumbled, obviously trying very hard to be serious.

"Well, you keep telling me you just sell sporting goods. I don't mean to question your veracity—after all, you are the man I love and have every intention of marrying. But Zack, I really would like to know how you intend to support this family of yours, especially all those brothers and sisters you promised Theresa!"

"Hmm," he said, sounding severe. "This'll teach you to question your husband's veracity. I will have you know that I do, in fact, sell sporting goods. Ever hear of—"

"*London's!*" she said, sitting upright and turning in his arms to stare at him. "Oh, my . . . word. That's you? London's Sporting Goods? I don't know why I didn't make the connection. I always thought that meant the *city.* Is that really *you?*"

"Us," he corrected her, hauling her back into his arms.

There was a thump and a low whistle, followed by a muted explosion. Star-bursts lit up the summer sky and cascaded down like sparkling rain.

Theresa cried "Oooh . . ." in wonder and delight, and then, with triumphant glee, "Maddy, I see Zack *kissing* you!"

Maddy erupted into helpless giggles.

"Get used to it, squirt," Zack growled. "Real parents do that a *lot!*"

As he reclaimed Maddy's mouth, skyrockets exploded again, *some* of them in the sky. . . .

THE EDITOR'S CORNER

Home for the Holidays! Certainly home is the nicest place to be in this upcoming season . . . and coming home, finding a home, perfecting one are key elements in each of our LOVESWEPTs next month.

First, in Peggy Webb's delightful **SCAMP OF SALTILLO,** LOVESWEPT #170, the heroine is setting up a new home in a small Mississippi town. Kate Midland is a witty, lovely, committed woman whose determination to save a magnolia tree imperiled by a construction crew brings her into face-to-face confrontation with Saltillo's mayor, Ben Adams. What a confrontation! What a mayor! Ben is self-confident, sensual, funny, generous . . . and perfect for Kate. But it takes a wacky mayoral race—including goats, bicycles, and kisses behind the bandstand—to bring these two fabulous people together. A romance with real heart and humor!

It is their homes—adjacent apartments—that bring together the heroine and hero in **FINNEGAN'S HIDEAWAY,** LOVESWEPT #171, by talented Sara Orwig. Lucy Reardon isn't really accident prone, but try to convince Finn Mundy of that. From the moment he spots the delectable-looking Lucy, her long, long shapely legs in black net stockings, he is falling . . . for her, with her, even

(continued)

off a ladder on top of her! But what are a few bruises, a minor broken arm compared to the enchantment and understanding Lucy offers? When Finn's brothers—and even his mother—show up on the doorstep, the scene is set for some even wilder misunderstandings and mishaps as Finn valiantly tries to handle that mob, his growing love for Lucy, law school exams, and his failing men's clothing business. A real charmer of a love story!

In the vivid, richly emotional **INHERITED,** LOVE-SWEPT #172, by gifted Marianne Shock, home is the source of a great deal of the conflict between heroine Tricia Riley and hero Chase Colby. Tricia's father hires Texas cowboy Chase to run Tricia's Virginia cattle ranch. Their attraction is instantaneous, explosive . . . as powerful as their apprehensions about sharing the running of the ranch. He brings her the gift of physical affection, for she was a child who lost her mother early in life and had never known her father's embrace or sweet words. She gives Chase the gift of emotional freedom and, at last, he can confide feelings he's never shared. But before these two ardent, needy people can come together both must deal with their troublesome pasts. A love story you'll cherish!

In **EMERALD FIRE,** LOVESWEPT #173, that marvelous storyteller Nancy Holder gives us a delightful couple in Stacy Livingston and Keith

(continued)

Mactavish . . . a man and a woman who seem worlds apart but couldn't be more alike at heart. And how does "home" play a part here? For both Stacy and Keith home means roots—his are in the exotic land of Hawaii, where ancestors and ancient gods are part of everyday life. Stacy has never felt she had any real roots, and has tried to find them in her work toward a degree as a marine biologist. Keith opens his arms and his home to her, sharing his large and loving family, his perceptions of sensual beauty and the real romance of life. You'll relish this exciting and provocative romance!

Home for the Holidays . . . in every heartwarming LOVESWEPT romance next month. Enjoy. And have a wonderful Thanksgiving celebration in your home!

Warm wishes,

Carolyn Nichols

Carolyn Nichols
    Editor
LOVESWEPT
Bantam Books, Inc.
666 Fifth Avenue
New York, NY 10103